Books by John Westin

The Anchor War
Stealing the White House
The Spy Book
The Perfect Candidate

THE PERFECT CANDIDATE

JOHN WESTIN

McNeil & Richards

Published by McNeil & Richards
www.mcneilandrichards.com

ISBN 13   978-0-9825602-8-0
ISBN   0-9825602-8-1

for Tony and Margaret

Acknowledgments

Judith Harris of Peoria IL and
Don Watson of Bethany OK
for German translation assistance

Contents

I

Goodbye
Morton Searcy

1

Murray Denton lifted a pack of Harry Jerome collector cards out of the cardboard box on his desk and tore off the blue and gold wrapper. He rubbed his fingers lightly over the cards, feeling the slick, glossy coating. Then he shuffled through them. George Madden was right. Madden's company had produced classy cards—every bit as good as the best sports and non-sports cards distributed by Upper Deck or Fleer. Stamped in gold foil on each card was the "Harry Jerome" logo. In this pack, cards depicted Harry rushing for a touchdown at San Jose State University, posing with his wife a few years before she died in a car crash on a West German autobahn, shaking hands with John Wayne, working in his office at the Farrell Foundation in Peoria, saving the life of a convenience store cashier by taking a bullet in the shoulder, and giving a "thumbs up" after his primary victory.

The only thing missing was the gum, mused Denton. In

the 1950s, most packs of cards came with slabs of bubble gum. Nevertheless, the cards were beauties, and if Jerome one day became a senator, or President of the United States, they would be worth a small fortune.

Denton set the cards aside on his cluttered desk and loosened his tie. He was tired. Managing Jerome's campaign for governor of Illinois was taking its toll. In the old days, Denton could work from seven in the morning until midnight without a break, but as the years passed he lost a lot of stamina and more than a little of his black hair. Now, at fifty-two, he owned the Eulenco Consulting Group in Springfield, Illinois, and he let younger staffers do most of the campaign grunt work.

Over the years, Denton had managed a dozen campaigns. He thought he had seen it all, but the Jerome campaign was different. It wasn't just the collector cards. There were other unusual and troubling things about the campaign.

Denton set aside the cards and began composing on his Dell computer a memo outlining campaign spending priorities. A few minutes later, his phone rang.

"Murray? ... "

It was her—the campaign's mole in the enemy camp. She was whispering. Her voice was throaty and seductive, like Lauren Bacall's. She talked a good game, lacing her speech with sexual innuendoes, but the promise of sexual ecstasy was an empty one. Despite her voluptuous figure and the hints at foreplay, she was all business. Ask her about work and she'd gab for hours. Try to get her in the sack and she'd turn so cold you'd think hell had frozen over. But that voice ... listening to her and imagining what could happen almost made up for everything else.

"... You've got a big problem. One of your people visited

my office today. Said he could blow the lid off Jerome's campaign."

"*What? Who was it?*"

"Morton Searcy."

"Searcy? That hayseed? Where did he find the guts to cross me?"

"But, Murray, he's good in bed."

Denton felt his blood pressure rising. She wouldn't give Denton the time of day but she got it on with Searcy?

"Wonderful," he groused.

She laughed softly. "Murray ... You didn't really think I'd let that twerp into my bed?"

"I don't know what you'd let into your bed."

"Don't be nasty, Murray ... Morton said he'd be back tomorrow, but he's nervous. Who knows what he'll do? Better take care of the problem."

Searcy's defection would mean big trouble for Denton. Searcy was a computer hacker who had played a key role in Harry's campaign. Searcy was a genius, and the problem with geniuses was that Denton never knew what they were up to. They could sell Eulenco lock, stock and barrel to a corporate raider without Denton knowing what the hell they were doing. Denton suspected something had irritated Searcy—perhaps something someone had said, or a rebuff when he asked for more pay, or sleepless nights caused by a guilty conscience—but the instigating event didn't really matter. The situation was critical. Searcy knew the campaign's dirtiest secrets.

Denton would have preferred to fire Searcy and let it go at that, but that was not an option. Searcy knew too much. He could not be trusted. Denton had his orders: if a problem arose, he was to notify Roger Moss, the man the campaign big shots had installed as security chief for Eulenco and the campaign. Moss would take care of the problem. Denton wasn't sure what Moss would do, but there was a lot at stake.

Denton reached for the phone.

"Moss? ... One of my people, Morton Searcy, has been poking into things he shouldn't. Find out what he knows and take care of the problem."

Roger Moss, a hulking bear of a man and former professional wrestler, relied on high-tech surveillance equipment and trained operatives to ensure that Harry Jerome's campaign ran smoothly. Although Denton had misgivings about the elaborate security setup, Moss had none. He loved it. Sitting behind the array of video monitors and control buttons, he could imagine he was Captain Kirk of the Starship Enterprise, exercising the power of life and death not only over people, but over entire planets.

Moss headed up a small Eulenco security force, but for messy jobs he didn't want tied to Jerome or Eulenco he used two freelancers—covert operatives who could be counted on to keep their mouths shut. Joey Randall was polished, efficient and professional. He hung out in fancy restaurants, luxury hotels and exclusive bars. The other freelancer, Wolfman, was primitive, brutal and emotional. He had a wild streak and was hard to control. He preferred dives and fleabag motels. When Moss needed help, he looked to Randall first.

Moss reached for his phone.

"Got a job for you, Randall. One of our people, Morton Searcy, is getting nosey. Take care of the problem."

"You mean permanently?"

"Affirmative."

"What's the time frame?"

"Do it *tonight*."

"So what'll you have? For five grand, I'll gun down your victim on a dark street. It'll look like a holdup."

"Someone might ask questions. This has gotta look like an accident."

"How about a fatal crash on the interstate? Very tidy."

"How much?" Moss inquired.

"Ten grand."

"Ten? I thought it was eight!"

"Inflation. What can I say?"

"What else?"

Randall sighed. "Look, this works best when you tell me who you want whacked and you leave the details to me. I need space to do my own thing."

"O.K., Rembrandt. Take care of it. But don't screw it up!"

"This is me you're talking to, Moss, not that social misfit Wolfman. The job will be done!"

Randall slammed the phone down. "Peasant," he mumbled.

"Psycho," Moss muttered. A simple job, and Randall wanted to make a DeMille production out of it.

Twenty minutes later, Randall arrived at Eulenco. Morton Searcy was still in the building. Moss had arranged for a Eulenco security man to show Randall a photo of Searcy taken from the traitor's personnel file.

"Kind of ugly," observed Randall. "A geek. He's asking for it."

Randall waited patiently for Searcy to leave Eulenco. At forty three, Randall still had most of his dark brown hair, and he considered himself handsome in a tough, Humphrey

Bogart kind of way. An avid James Bond fan, he was decked out in a two-piece gray suit, as usual, and had a decanter of scotch on the seat next to him. You've gotta go through life first class, Randall believed. Let the Morton Searcys and Roger Mosses save bucks by going coach.

Given his views on operating with style, Randall was understandably embarrassed to be sitting in a beat up Ford station wagon. He hated using it on jobs, but his girlfriend had the Cadillac. Maybe it was a good thing. Searcy wouldn't think anyone would be stupid enough to follow him in a station wagon the size of a small house.

At 7:46, Searcy left the building by a side entrance and headed straight for a green Datsun. Randall had no trouble spotting him.

Through darkened streets, Randall followed Searcy at a distance, using a cell phone to keep in contact with Delphi—Moss' name for home base of the Eulenco security operation.

"What's the latest, Randall?" Moss asked.

"The pigeon is heading northwest."

"Must be going home."

"Affirmative," Randall said. "Nothing suspicious."

Thirteen minutes later, Searcy arrived at his two-story wooden frame house on West Lawrence Street. Randall parked the wagon a half block away.

"He's home, Delphi. I'm goin' in. In five minutes, he'll be on his way to Turncoat Heaven."

"You worry me, Randall."

"This is reality, baby. Wake up and smell the donuts."

Randall placed the phone on the car seat and headed for Searcy's house.

Randall planned to force his way inside the house and confront Searcy, but before Randall reached the driveway, Searcy dashed out of the house, hopped into his Datsun and roared off. Randall hustled back to the station wagon, revved up the engine and picked up his cell phone. "We're rolling again, Delphi."

"That was fast. Maybe something's going on."

Randall trailed Searcy as the renegade hacker sped along Walnut Street to the northwestern edge of Springfield. It became obvious Searcy was heading for Capitol Airport.

Things were not going smoothly.

"What should I do, Moss?"

Back at Delphi, Moss mulled his options. They were limited. If Searcy was flying somewhere for a rendezvous with state or federal law enforcement officers, he had to be stopped. Collateral damage was probably inevitable.

"Eliminate the problem," ordered Moss.

Searcy pulled into the long-term parking area and hurried inside the airport terminal. Randall followed at a distance. Searcy glanced furtively from side to side as he approached the ticket counter. By the time Searcy reached the head of the line, Randall was behind him. Searcy purchased a ticket for a Chicago flight that would depart in twenty minutes.

Randall returned to his station wagon, grabbed a few tools out of the back and cautiously made his way to the commuter plane that would carry Searcy to Chicago. When Moss was sure no one was watching, he went to work.

II

The Bashful Candidate

2

13 days before the election

Palm trees swayed in the sultry Fort Lauderdale breeze and waves crashed along the shore as David McGraw whipped his blue Corvette along A1A. He had overslept. Instead of cruising along at his usual leisurely pace, McGraw pushed the accelerator to the floor. If he covered the distance from his apartment to the *National Exposer* offices in record time, he could put in a full hour of work before lunch. Maybe it was the workaholic in him, but he decided to go for it.

A minute and forty-three seconds after leaving his apartment, the twenty-eight-year-old journalist pulled into the parking lot abutting a seedy stucco building nestled behind a rotting palm tree. A few moments later, so did News Editor Walter Boylan, a cigar-chomping New Yorker who happened to be McGraw's boss.

McGraw decided to beat Boylan to the punch.

"You're late!" McGraw snapped. "I've been out looking for you the last two hours."

"Stow it, McGraw. I got into the office about 8:30. I just took off a few minutes to grab a cup of coffee. But I appreciate you showing up before lunch."

"No problem, Walter. It's the least I can do."

McGraw threw an arm around Boylan's shoulder as they sauntered into the building. "What are the chances of taking an early lunch?"

"Pretty good for me. Lousy for you."

"I may complain about the working conditions."

"Won't do any good," Boylan said. "The publisher is in Bermuda this week."

A half hour later, McGraw looked up from the computer where he had been fine-tuning a headline and gazed out the window. On the other side of A1A, tourists trudged along a sandy beach. Seagulls swooped down from overhead. The sky had cleared after a morning shower, and the sun was shining brightly.

Gregarious and impulsive, McGraw was one of three copy editors who whipped stories into shape for the *National Exposer*, a tabloid rag that contaminated supermarket checkout racks throughout North America. About a million people shelled out a dollar and eighty nine cents for the *Exposer* each week to read stories like the one McGraw was wrestling with:

**ALIENS KIDNAP
OPRAH WINFREY;
SHE'LL RUN JUPITER**

Although some of the country's uninhibited supermarket

weeklies had moved their offices to New York, the *Exposer* still operated out of Florida.

Walter Boylan peeked at McGraw's computer screen. "Try 'Mars'," he suggested. "It fits better than 'Jupiter'."

"The story says she's going to run Jupiter," McGraw protested.

"Change the story, too. Good grief, McGraw. Don't worry about accuracy in a yarn like this."

The copydesk phone rang. Boylan reached for it.

"Line 1, McGraw. Someone named Slater."

McGraw couldn't believe the state editor of the *Chicago Chronicle* was calling. Rick Slater rarely spoke to McGraw when McGraw worked for him. Why did he want to talk to McGraw now?

"How would you like to come back to beautiful, sunny Chicago?" Slater asked with forced cheerfulness.

McGraw knew that Slater, a harried man in his late forties, was a cantankerous workaholic who feigned friendliness only when he wanted something. McGraw also was aware the weather report in that morning's *Fort Lauderdale News* indicated Chicago would have a rainy day, with a high of forty-six.

"You've got to be kidding," McGraw snapped. "It took me twenty-seven years to get out of Chicago."

"Don't be hasty, McGraw. You know you're wasting your time at that crummy rag. I've never understood how a reporter can look at himself in the mirror when he works at a piece of crap like the *Exposer*."

Slater was right about that. Working for supermarket tabloids had many advantages—the higher pay and Florida's balmy climate came to mind—but there was one rather significant disadvantage: every time McGraw wrote a head-line or edited a story at the *Exposer* he had the feeling he was selling a little more of his soul. McGraw missed the respectability and prestige of working for a reputable news-paper. In Chicago, people were impressed when he told them where he worked: "Wow! You work for the *Chronicle!*" In Florida, the reaction was different: "Dear God! You work for the *Exposer*?"

"I'm offering you a way out, McGraw. Got a job for you. I can't go into details on the phone, but there could be a helluva story involving a candidate for governor. It'll take some digging, but it could be a career maker! I'm will-ing to forget you couldn't cut it here and give you another chance."

That got McGraw's dander up. "Couldn't cut it? Why, you has-been. I carried you for five years! You would have been fired long ago if I hadn't saved your ass."

"That's not the way I remember it. But what's past is past. Forget it. Just quit your screwing around and get back here! I need somebody *now*. The election is less than two weeks away."

"I don't understand why you're calling me," McGraw said. "You always hated my guts."

"Nonsense. What gave you that idea?"

"You told me you did, thirty or forty times."

"Well, sure, but I didn't mean it. I wanted to motivate you ... push you to do a better job."

"You must be in a real jam if you're asking me to come back."

A voice in McGraw's head whispered, "Don't be a sap, McGraw. Slater is a slave driver. Give up Florida to work for that jerk? No way, José."

McGraw leaned back in his second-hand swivel chair and gazed out the window at a shy tourist of college age who seemed to be debating whether to take off her jacket and bare all that her skimpy bikini would allow. She hesitated, started to take off the jacket, then thought better of it and slipped it back on. Still hanging onto the phone, McGraw leaned over to the open window.

"Do it, honey! Go for it! You're not going to have that body forever!"

Startled and embarrassed, the girl hugged her jacket tightly around her and hurried back to her Thunderbird.

"What are you yelling about, McGraw?"

"I thought I saw your wife across the street," McGraw lied.

"Can't be Myrna. She's in a de-tox center. Says I drove her to drink. That's ridiculous. I haven't driven her anywhere in months. ... Look, McGraw, you've heard the deal. I'm trying to do you a big favor. Just say 'yes' so I don't waste any more of my time. I've got a paper to get out."

Slater was always impatient—a Type-A heart attack candidate. He couldn't connect with the laid-back Florida lifestyle. He was chained to a desk all day and under a lot of stress, and like other *Chronicle* staffers, he wore sport coats and ties to work. At the *Exposer*, no one minded that McGraw chose to wear jeans and a dirty sweatshirt bearing the message "Let's Get Down and Dirty".

"Thanks, Slater, but I couldn't possibly tear myself away from writing headlines like 'WEREWOLF STUFFS SLY STALLONE INTO TRASH CAN'. Find yourself another pigeon. I've gotta go. I'm on a tight schedule. I've got to whip up a few slanderous headlines, lick some shit off the editor's shoes and run down to the beach to leer at Big

Rosie. She's a free-spirited nymphomaniac who wears biki-nis two sizes too small for her. But take care, you hear?"

"McGraw, wait! Don't hang up! ... Are you there, McGraw?"

McGraw sighed. "I'm here."

"Look, hotshot, stories like this don't come down the pike every day. This is a great opportunity, and there's a raise in it for you. This is your chance to get out of that swamp of mediocre fiction and lurid headlines. Come back to the real world! ... And there's another thing you might consider. If you don't help me, I'll see to it that you never work for a legitimate newspaper again!"

"You always were an asshole," McGraw grumbled. "Hang on a minute." He turned to Boylan, who was flip-ping through a folder in search of a recent photo of Big Foot. "My old boss in Chicago is offering me a job, Walter. Says if I turn him down, I'll never work for a legit paper again."

Boylan shrugged. "I thought *this* was a legit paper and everyone else was doing it wrong. ... Hell, take the job. You can always come back to Paradise and sewer journalism if you have to."

"All right," McGraw told Slater. "I'll be in Chicago in a few days."

"You'll be in Chicago *tonight*," Slater growled. "I'll see you at the office first thing in the morning. What do you think we're running here—a weekly?"

McGraw hung up. "I want to quit the *Chronicle* already," he mumbled.

"Better get out your snow shovel." Boylan suggested. "You must be nuts going back to Chicago and all that snow and ice."

"But you told me to!"

"Yeah, but I didn't think you'd be dumb enough to do it. You're too naive to work here. Go on, go back to the big, windy, cold city. And don't worry about Big Rosie. I'll tell her goodbye for you as we're sipping mai tais on the beach."

3

A TWA jumbo jet carrying McGraw and 132 other passengers arrived at O'Hare International Airport at eight that evening.

In the baggage area, an airline employee informed McGraw his suitcase was on its way to Hawaii. Why did the luggage always have more exciting destinations than the passengers? Well, it didn't matter because McGraw had outwitted the luggage handlers. He had stuffed old clothes into a dummy suitcase—the one that was on its way to Hawaii—and had packed a few of his best clothes in the overnight bag he kept with him on the plane.

It was only after he checked into the Hyatt Regency downtown that he discovered he had grabbed the wrong overnight bag and someone six inches shorter whose taste in shirts was ludicrous had McGraw's clothes. McGraw's Law: if they're going to get you, they're going to get you no matter what you do. It applied to women, too.

McGraw decided he would spend his first evening back in Chicago looking up some of his old friends. After shaving and washing up, he rode a bus to Chicago's Near North Side and got off at Clark Street, about five blocks from the brick apartment building where he had lived during his first stint at the *Chronicle*. Chilly breezes off Lake Michigan swirled McGraw's dark brown hair as he headed north on Clark, passing Lincoln Park.

The walk brought back memories. The Near North Side was his favorite part of the city, though it cost an arm and a leg to rent an apartment there and you had about as much chance of finding a decent parking space as you did of winning fifteen million in the state lottery. But if you wanted to live in the Near North Side, you had to take the bad with the good. Residents discovered that in 1871 when the Great Chicago Fire leveled nearly everything in that part of the city.

It was a more dynamic area than suburban Morton Grove, where McGraw's parents had lived before they moved to Wisconsin and where he had spent his childhood. Even late in the evening, Clark Street was bustling. One of the friendlier residents called out to McGraw:

"What the hell you doin', asshole? Why you lookin' at ma car like that?"

"I wasn't looking at your car, I was looking at your girlfriend," McGraw snarled. It was probably the wrong thing to say to someone who was a few shingles short of a roof.

McGraw hurried on, passing quaint shops, trendy bars and ethnic restaurants before arriving at Morelli's, a small restaurant tucked between a hot dog stand and a drugstore on Fullerton Avenue.

Morelli's had been McGraw's favorite haunt before he left Chicago. Pete Morelli and his wife, Gina, were Italian-Americans who still believed in the American dream, even when times got so bad they could barely eke out a living. Their daughter Maria was a beguiling twenty-six-year-old who waited on tables. She had married young and was divorced. McGraw and Maria had dated and rolled around in the sack a few times, but she dumped him before it turned into anything serious.

McGraw passed a half dozen tables covered with white-and-red checkered tablecloths before sitting at a small table near the kitchen—and Maria.

Pete Morelli, tall and heavy-set, a gregarious man with curly black hair, emerged from the kitchen carrying a bottle of Chianti. His face curled into a smile when he realized McGraw was back at his old table.

"Hey, it's the reporter!" Morelli said. "Thought you moved to Florida, McGraw."

"I'm back. The *Chronicle* couldn't get along without me."

Morelli chuckled. "That scandal sheet in Florida fired you, didn't they? I knew you were one of them floaters. You just float from job to job."

"I wasn't fired. The *Chronicle* said they needed me to cover a big story. So I came back."

"Needed you … that's a good one," Morelli grumbled, as he placed the wine on a nearby table where an elderly man wrestled with a plate of spaghetti.

McGraw was about to defend his reputation when Maria waltzed in from the kitchen. Her soft black hair glittered in the light. She was more buxom than he remembered.

"McGraw! What are you doing back here?"

"I took a wrong turn on Ocean Boulevard and wound up in Chicago. Weren't we scheduled to go out tonight?"

"I don't think so. Has hell frozen over?"

Morelli laughed.

"Such foul language. Morelli, you didn't do a very good job of raising Maria."

"Yes, I did. She only uses language like that around you."

Maria leaned over to wipe the table. McGraw's eyes were drawn to her bosom.

"You want a menu?" she asked.

"That, and anything else you've got."

"Don't talk to my daughter like that!," Morelli warned. "She's young and impressionable."

"She was married at sixteen," McGraw noted. "She knows more about the facts of life than Madonna. Besides, if she isn't interested, she shouldn't wipe off tables. She turns it into an erotic experience."

Morelli grimaced. "Enough, McGraw. Put it in neutral. I've heard about you reporters."

"Amen," chimed in Burt Reardon, a cop who had just wandered over to McGraw's table. "I'd send my daughter naked into the ghettoes before I'd let her go out with a reporter."

Reardon seated himself.

"You haven't got a daughter," McGraw noted.

"That's not the point," Reardon said. "If I had one, and she dated a reporter, I'd throw her out of the house."

McGraw ordered the ravioli, Reardon the lasagna.

"What's goin' on, McGraw?" Reardon asked. "Couldn't stand Paradise?"

Morelli shrugged. "McGraw says they called him back to cover a big story. Second Coming, or something like that."

Reardon chuckled. "That's a good one."

Reardon told McGraw about his latest drug bust—he had nabbed three old-timers for using drugs. How was he supposed to know they were prescription medicines?

A few minutes later, Maria served the ravioli and lasagna.

"We've missed the stories about your Romantic Encounters From Hell," Reardon said. "Have any better luck in Florida?"

"I was hanging out with Big Rosie, but she's not wife material. She's the kind of woman you hide in the closet when your mother visits."

"That's disgusting," Maria muttered, as she marched off to the kitchen.

"Not to me," Reardon said. "If I go down to Florida on vacation, could you fix me up with Rosie?"

"You don't need to be fixed up," McGraw assured him. "If she sees you on the beach, she'll be all over you in about ten seconds."

"Why aren't there women like that around here?" Morelli mused.

"There are, but they charge by the hour," Reardon pointed out.

Morelli switched on the old Sylvania television near the cash register. On Channel 8, a half-hour infomercial was winding down. Sue Ellen Jerrell, a vivacious extrovert who could sell a trainload of sirloin steaks to vegetarians, recapped for viewers why they should fork out $249 to learn the secrets that would bring them wealth beyond their wildest dreams ...

"So what's it going to be? Will you spend the rest of your life slouched on a couch dreaming about what could have been, or will you take your fate into your own hands and embark on a new life

today? The decision is yours! Don't come whining to me in two or three years saying, 'Sue Ellen, why didn't I listen to you? Why didn't I start earning hundreds of thousands of dollars back then instead of ignoring your advice and flicking the dial to a re-run of a third-rate sitcom?'

"This is your wake-up call. People in all walks of life have purchased my cassettes, and they are making money with a capital M!"

Reardon rummaged through his pockets. "McGraw— you got two-hundred-forty-nine bucks you can spare?"

"Are you kidding? I spend my money as fast as I get it."

Reardon's eyes lit up. "There ... the 800 number's on the screen! Write it down! ... Hurry! Write down the number!"

By the time Reardon, Morelli and McGraw found a pencil and a napkin to write on, the number had disappeared from the screen and the show was over.

"Now you've done it," Reardon growled. "My shot at success just went down the toilet—all because of you, McGraw! You couldn't loan me a measly two-hundred-and-forty-nine bucks. I won't forget this! I could be making out with Sue Ellen in a home worth five hundred grand instead of pounding a beat."

The infomercial gave way to Channel 8's local news, anchored by amiable, fast-talking Ralph Benton.

"... and the victim is in stable condition.

"In other news, Chicago-based media tycoon Martin Hudson arrived today in Singapore, where he's battling two other communication conglomerates in a bidding war for a satellite TV operation. Singapore has about three million residents, but it is positioning itself as the communications hub for a region with three billion people. Even so, the satellite operation is small potatoes compared to the billion-dollar global communications/

entertainment complex Hudson sought to build in Illinois. Governor Dodge killed that deal by refusing to support loans and loan guarantees for Hudson."

"Has Big Rosie been busted for soliciting?" Reardon wondered.

"She spends more time in the Lauderdale police station than the cops do," McGraw noted.

"The governor and Attorney General Betsy Kimball hit the campaign trail today in Rockford, where the governor defended his decision to block the loan guarantees."

Film showed the governor speaking at a League of Women Voters meeting in Rockford.

"Some powerful interests in the state would make huge profits if the Hudson Entertainment and Communications Center is built, but my responsibility is to the public—not the fat cats. I can not justify spending tens of millions of taxpayer dollars on a project that belongs entirely in the private sector!"

Benton appeared on the screen again.

"A Chicago Chronicle *poll released today shows the governor's race is the tightest in years. With two weeks remaining before the election, Governor Dodge now leads challenger Harry Jerome by only one percentage point!"*

"Dodge had better watch it," Morelli said. "He could get his ass kicked."

"Meanwhile, Jerome told a crowd of about four hundred in Joliet that Dodge's 'corrupt, complacent and incompetent' administration is taxing business out of the state. And, Jerome committed another major blunder today …"

Film showing Jerome working the crowd rolled. The candidate appeared handsome and vigorous. His dyed brown hair made him look much younger than his fifty-four years. McGraw noted Jerome was wearing a silk suit that probably cost a thousand bucks.

"Crime has reached epidemic proportions. Something must be done! If I am elected, I would not hesitate to order National Guard troops to patrol Chicago streets to round up criminals!"

"Is he nuts?" McGraw asked. "Why would he talk about sending troops into Chicago?"

Benton continued ...

"Jerome's press secretary, Duncan Jamieson, later issued a clarification saying Jerome merely was reiterating that he believes strongly in law and order. He does not believe it would ever be necessary to call out Guardsmen to patrol the streets of Chicago. Well, that's a relief, isn't it, folks."

"And that's the intellectual giant who might be our next governor," Reardon muttered.

"This is the second time Jerome has created controversy by mis-speaking in the last week. Last Tuesday, he railed against 'freeloaders in the nursing homes'. He seemed to be condemning everyone in nursing homes. Political observers wonder if the campaign is taking its toll on Jerome, the Peoria foundation president who until recently seemed to lead a charmed political life."

"They shouldn't bad-mouth Jerome," Morelli said. "I like what he says about keeping the lid on taxes!"

"And he sure is handsome," Maria noted.

McGraw was annoyed. "Morelli, your daughter is love-sick over a politician twice her age!"

Morelli shrugged. "At least he ain't a reporter."

On his way back to the Hyatt Regency, McGraw concluded that seeing Maria again had been therapeutic, despite the damage to his ego. It suddenly became clear that the land-scape of his past was littered with wasted time and failed relationships. For years, he had associated with two types of females: (1) those who toyed with him, used him, and then cut him loose, and (2) women of Higher Standards who refused to even go out with him. That had to change. Now that he was starting a new job, it was time to cut his ties with the past. The New McGraw would be in control of his fate. The New McGraw would be confident, dynamic and assertive.

McGraw released a long sigh. If past experiences were any indication, the New McGraw was in for a long, cold, lonely winter.

4

At the Eulenco building in Springfield, Murray Denton rolled up his shirt sleeves, plopped his feet on his desk and pulled a remote control out of a desk drawer. He flicked on an RCA television nestled on a bookcase at the far end of his office. Closing credits for a cop show filled the screen.

Farley Johnson, the Eulenco research director, stuck his balding head inside Denton's office. "We've merged five more databases! I know everything there is to know about a helluva lot of the voters in this state—where they were born and went to school, credit history, church preference, where they work, how they feel about abortion, gun control and Palmolive soap … I tell you, Murray, they won't be able to take a crap without me knowing about it."

"Sometimes you scare me, Farley."

"Next, I plan to hook up miniature cameras in their homes … We'll buy a cable television company and stick the cameras inside the converter boxes … We'll make the movie channel fees so low no one can afford not to have them, and they'll be forced to use the scrambler boxes. Soon, there will be hidden cameras inside hundreds of thousands of homes across the state. If anyone even thinks about voting the wrong way, we'll know about it."

Denton sighed. "Promise me you'll take a long rest after the election, Farley."

"No time to rest, Murray! There's work to be done!"

As Farley hurried back to his office to hunt for more databases to rape, Denton mulled over the information Farley had just given him. Merging scores of databases had been one of the goals of the campaign planners. The more information about potential voters, the better. Mailings could be targeted to their needs and interests more precisely than ever before. People could be manipulated and controlled more easily than ever before. Even so, Farley seemed to be taking things a bit far.

On television, the Channel 10 News began. Marilyn Westley, a perky blonde reporter, described Harry Jerome's latest attack of foot-in-mouth disease.

"Jerome still trails Governor Dodge in the polls, but Jerome has taken the lead in one category—blunders on the campaign trail. He racked up another one today in Joliet when he told several hundred supporters that crime has reached epidemic proportions and, if elected, he would not hesitate to send troops into the streets of Chicago to round up criminals, if necessary. Jerome's aides turned pale when they heard that campaign promise."

"Harry's out of his ever-lovin' mind," Denton grumbled.

Denton reached for the phone and called Harry's press secretary, Duncan Jamieson, in Galesburg, Jerome's latest stop. Jamieson said the candidate was about to leave for a fund-raising dinner.

"What's the matter with Harry?" Denton demanded.

"We can't win if he looks like a fool every time he opens his mouth!"

"He's exhausted," Jamieson said.

"Who isn't? He's got to understand he can't screw up like that! Let me talk to him."

The candidate came on the line. "Murray! How's tricks, you old rascal?"

"Have you been drinking, Harry?"

"Only the liquor of life!"

"How much of the liquor of life have you had today?"

"Oh, three highballs. Maybe four."

"Are you nuts? You've got to keep a clear head!"

"If I kept a clear head, I couldn't function at all. A highball or two keeps me going. Lets me forget my troubles and the sad state of the world."

"All right, Harry. What's wrong? What's buggin' you?"

"What could possibly be wrong? My right hand is numb from pumping the clammy paws of politicians, my speechwriter is running out of proposals to make the lives of the poor even more miserable, and I spend hours every day cooped up in a Chrysler with Jamieson and the other hotshots you've assigned to babysit me. I've gained twenty pounds over the last few months because I've eaten two hundred chickens, a hundred steaks and a hundred fish dinners. My cholesterol count is probably about nine hundred."

"Now, Harry …"

"I'm not kidding. Ripley wants to list me in the next *Believe It Or Not* book."

"Behave yourself, Harry. You can't fall apart on us now! You can rest after the election!"

Harry gritted his teeth. "Another two weeks of chicken dinners."

"And let me remind you, Harry, that you are *not* to mingle with the press. Your remark the other day about 'making crippies more productive' probably cost us several thousand votes. The handicapped don't like to be called 'crippies'. They're the 'physically challenged'. And don't dish out any more of that crap about how great it was growing up in Ukiah, California. The less said about Ukiah—and anything else—the better. Get your head on straight. This isn't a game! ... Let me talk to your mentally challenged press secretary again."

Harry put Jamieson on the line.

"Yeah, Murray."

"We can't afford any more screwups. Keep Harry away from reporters! Let him deliver his speeches and get out of there. I'll cancel a couple appearances to give him some rest, but we've only got two weeks 'til the election. He's got to bite the bullet and do his job!"

"I know, Murray. I'll tell him."

"And one more thing. Harry's coming across as too tough. Sure, we want people to think he can handle the job, but if he isn't sensitive and likeable, no one will vote for him. There's too much of the attack dog in Harry, not enough of the shaggy dog. Do you understand what I'm saying?"

"Sure. You want him to smile when he talks about throwing old ladies into prison."

"Don't toy with me, Duncan. I've had a tough day."

"No—I've got it! You want him to hand out cookies and cake after he talks about how rough corporate CEOs have it."

"You're treading on thin ice, Duncan. I'm warning you—get things under control! ... I tell you what ... you'll be in

Peoria the next couple days. I'll drive up there to make sure everything goes smoothly."

Denton hung up.

Susan Noles, a pollster who was working late, stuck her head in Denton's office. "We're up three points in Champaign-Urbana. Dead heat with Dodge!"

"Harry must have grabbed his arm again," Denton suggested. It was a standing joke around Eulenco that whenever Harry was slipping, he could get gain ground in the polls by clutching the arm wounded by the convenience store holdup man, a thug named Pete Lorton, four months earlier. That incident had marked the turning point in Harry's campaign, making him a hero and a celebrity and carrying him to an easy victory in the primary. And it was still good for votes.

A half hour later, Roger Moss burst into Denton's office carrying computer printouts.

"Searcy left a present behind for you, Denton. A little time bomb that could ruin everything."

Denton glared at his security chief. "What are you talking about?"

Moss sat down and handed Denton the printouts. "Randall found these in the briefcase Searcy had with him when he bought the farm."

Denton flipped through the papers. "I don't get it. We never went into this much detail on Jerome's background. We decided to keep it simple."

"It ain't simple anymore. ... Searcy helped create Harry's background, didn't he?"

"That's right," Denton said.

"Well, I checked out the details in these printouts. *They're all true!*"

"What do you mean they're all true? We created Harry!"

"You thought Searcy made up a background for your candidate. But Searcy was a lazy sunuvabitch. He took a real guy and used the details of his life. There really was a Harry Jerome. He died sixteen years ago!"

"That isn't possible!" Denton insisted.

"It's all in here. Hell, I thought you were running a fictitious candidate for governor—but you're running a dead man!"

Denton skimmed the printouts. "If Searcy was on his way to deliver this, someone knows something's up. They don't have the details, but they know where to start digging. We told people Harry lived in Ukiah and attended San Jose State. Send Randall to California to tie up any loose ends. See if Harry has any relatives we need to send into hiding. Get rid of any public records or newspaper articles mentioning his death that people are likely to find. If anyone digs into Harry's background, they'll find only what we want them to find. ... We can control this, Moss, and we can do it without more killing! Nineteen people died in that plane crash!"

Moss pulled himself out of the seat like a general defending his honor. "I had my orders, and I carried them out as I saw fit!"

"Use restraint! You could go to the chair for killing those people!

"We all could, Denton."

Denton was shocked. "What are you talking about? It was *your* decision. Randall followed your orders!"

Moss leaned across Denton's desk and glared menacingly. "Whether you like it or not, Denton, *you* are as responsible for those nineteen deaths as Randall is. Don't forget that!"

"Don't try to shift the blame to me, Moss. I simply told you there was a problem. I'm a political consultant, not a murderer."

"You told me to take care of the problem. And I did."

Denton mopped his brow with a handkerchief. "Well, when you take care of *this* problem, tell your men to show restraint!"

Moss headed for the door. "Some operation you have here. I'd like to hear you explain this to the people who hired you to run Harry's campaign."

"Just do your job, Moss."

Moss slammed the door on his way out.

Using the cell phone in his Dodge Charger, Moss called Randall.

"Start packing. You're flying to California. You've got to clean up a mess for us."

5

12 days before the election

With a sense of awe and reverence, McGraw entered the palatial lobby of the *Chronicle* building, one of the oldest skyscrapers on Chicago's Michigan Avenue. When it opened in the 1920s, the *Chronicle* was an aggressive, independent, defiant newspaper. Guided by its founder, David Bellingham, it crusaded against corruption on the news pages and railed against injustices on its editorial page. After Bellingham died in 1948, the paper coasted on its reputation while it became fatter, richer and more complacent, despite the best intentions of some of its editors and reporters.

McGraw rode a slow, refurbished elevator to the sprawling third-floor newsroom. He exchanged small talk with several reporters and scrutinized the newsroom bulletin board to see who was in trouble with the brass and who was licking the brass' boots. As he approached the State Desk at the north end of the building, he could see Rick Slater tapping away at his computer keyboard.

Slater was tall and lanky. His brown hair was speckled with gray, and his face was frozen in a perpetual grimace. To McGraw, Slater seemed like an android with a lousy personality. Although McGraw had never liked Slater, he respected him. Slater was as tough on himself as he was on his staff. He would trade his mother to savages if he thought he'd get a good story out of it. That wasn't McGraw's opinion. Slater had told him that.

McGraw planted himself in front of Slater's desk, a few feet away from the State Desk where copy from reporters and correspondents around the state was edited. Slater ignored McGraw, apparently determined to prove who was boss by keeping him waiting. After Slater edited and re-edited a story on his computer terminal, he acknowledged McGraw's presence.

"You're late, McGraw."

"I was here a half hour ago, but I didn't want to interrupt your nap."

"Look, McGraw, I hired you because we are desperate. I'm not going to put up with insubordination. You're a troublemaker, a loose wheel—"

"Cannon," McGraw interrupted. "They call me a 'loose cannon'."

"—and a smartass."

"That isn't what you said on the phone. What happened to 'we need you, McGraw—you're the best reporter we ever had and I'm dirt'?"

The State Desk copy editors looked at Slater in amazement.

"I never said that. I said 'if you're tired of screwing up on that scandal sheet, come back here and screw up for a while.' Besides, that was before you agreed to return. Now that you're here, I can treat you like moose crap."

The copy editors resumed working. *That* was the Slater they knew.

McGraw sighed. It was obvious Slater had not mellowed.

"And don't make yourself comfortable, McGraw. Go down to Personnel, fill out the forms Amy gives you, then report back to me. And make it fast!"

McGraw loosened his tie. "I've been thinking, Slater. I'm not sure I want to tramp around the state tracking down a story. Isn't there a cushy desk job I could have? A job like yours, that doesn't require any intelligence or ability?"

Slater glared at the infidel he had enticed back into the fold. "Get moving! You're already late!"

McGraw shuffled toward the elevator.

Managing Editor George Purnell approached Slater's desk. "Wasn't that—"

"McGraw," said Slater. "David McGraw."

"McGraw ... Didn't he quit the *Chronicle* to work for one of those supermarket rags in Florida?"

"That's right. He's back. I need him to cover Jerome's campaign."

"You're joking, right?"

Slater glared at Purnell. "No. McGraw did some pretty good reporting for the state desk, you know."

"He also had an attitude. Hard to keep in line. You actually rehired him?"

"What else could I do? I needed a reporter fast, and I haven't got time to break one in."

"But McGraw ... holy shit. I remember the day he left. I was so happy I got drunk."

"You get drunk three times a week, anyway."

"Yeah, but that night I had a reason. ... McGraw. Ye, gods."

As McGraw waited to be "processed" in the Personnel Department, the secretary—Amy—left the room. McGraw decided to alleviate his boredom by thumbing through files in a steel cabinet. He pulled Slater's dossier.

He learned that Richard Humboldt Slater was born in Waterloo, Iowa; attended schools in Waterloo; graduated from the Iowa State University with a degree in journalism; and handled reporting for a podunk paper in Clinton, Iowa, before joining the *Chronicle* as a reporter. He had worked for the *Chronicle* sixteen years, nine of them as state editor.

It was no secret in the newsroom that the ambitious Slater had his eyes on the managing editor job, but the executives who ran the *Chronicle* had ignored him. McGraw knew Slater was biding his time, making sure he did nothing to jeopardize his career at the *Chronicle* while waiting for his Big Break.

McGraw rummaged through Slater's file, finding a few juicy nuggets of information, until he heard Amy returning to her office. He hastily replaced the file.

After signing a W-2 withholding form and receiving a copy of the company's new health insurance plan, McGraw headed back to the State Desk.

"I was reading some of your old stories," Slater said. "I may have made a mistake, McGraw. You may not have what it takes to do investigative reporting."

"Those were stories you assigned me," McGraw pointed out. He leaned back in the chair. "Tell me, Slater: that nasty little incident six years ago, when you flunked the company's random drug testing. Were you really on medication, or were you flying high on coke?"

Slater's eyes opened wide. "Where did you hear that? No one's supposed to know that!"

"I was just using it as an illustration. I can dig for the facts when it's necessary."

Slater gulped. "Let's go into my office."

Slater's office was an eight-foot by eight-foot room crammed full of bookcases, books and newspapers. He seated himself behind the swayback desk and motioned for McGraw to sit in a straight back chair. "All right, McGraw. I'll fill you in on your assignment. Seven months ago Carl Yorbly, our reporter covering Harry Jerome's campaign for governor, injured his back on the same day Harry became a hero by taking a bullet in an arm. Ever since then, Yorbly complained of back pain. A couple days ago he was taken to the hospital. I think the surgery could have waited, but Yorbly is something of a baby about these things."

McGraw winced as he recalled the note on the *Chronicle* bulletin board describing how Yorbly, writhing in pain, was hauled to a hospital on a flat board. Slater was the kind of editor who expected you to work even if a surfboard was rammed through your chest, one end hanging out the front and the other out the back.

"Anyway, he'll be out of action until after the election. The state staff was cut to the bone by budget cuts. I don't have anyone to send downstate to cover Jerome. I can't break in a kid on this job. I need someone who knows his way around. That's where you come in."

McGraw's mouth fell open. He was stunned. He had read about Jerome—his convenience store heroism and primary victory—in the Florida papers, but Jerome was just another politician. Had McGraw given up a high-paying job a stone's throw from the beach in Florida—and Big Rosie—to birddog a lousy two-bit politician around Illinois?

"You don't need me!" McGraw bellowed. "Anyone could cover Jerome's campaign. I can't believe you did this to me! I thought you said there was a great story here!"

"Don't blow a gasket, McGraw. You're missing the big picture. This is no ordinary assignment. Jerome is only a point behind Governor Dodge in the polls, and he has momentum. He could be the next governor of Illinois—but no one knows anything about him! His backers have put up a protective wall around him. Jerome is running the most secretive, manipulative, carefully orchestrated campaign I've ever seen, and he's getting away with it."

Slater paused and gazed at the massive newsroom through his office window. "We've got to find out if Jerome is hiding something. ... And then there's the matter of Morton Searcy's death."

"Who's Morton Searcy?"

"Searcy worked for Eulenco, the consulting company handling Jerome's campaign. Searcy was killed when a commuter plane flying from Springfield to Chicago took a nose-dive into a cornfield. His body was found last week."

McGraw had read about the crash in the *Fort Lauderdale News*.

"The FAA says it looks like an accident—that an instrument malfunctioned," Slater said. "I'm not so sure. When rescuers arrived at the scene, a man was seen rummaging through Searcy's pockets."

"It could have been a looter."

"Looters don't usually wear suits." Slater pounded his desk with his right fist. "I tell you, McGraw, there's something strange about Jerome's whole campaign. We've got to find out what's going on before he's elected—and we have less than two weeks to do it. Twelve million residents of this state have a stake in this. No one else is doing the job. Martin Hudson's *Sentinel* and his television stations are throwing everything they have behind Jerome. That means it's up to you and me."

McGraw shook his head. "Good grief, Slater. That sounds like work."

"You'll be working your tail off, McGraw. News coverage of Jerome's campaign has been pathetic. No one's asking the tough questions. Yorbly's stories sounded like PR releases. You must do better. You've got to dig through the crap and get at the truth!"

Slater leaned across the desk. "Find out everything there is to know about Jerome—his qualifications for the job, what he's done with his life, what he believes in, what kind of man he is, who's backing him. Does he have a secret agenda? How does he think he can run the state if he refuses to raise taxes? Why is his campaign keeping his running mate, Karl Olson, on a short leash? And why the hell does Jerome act so squirrelly sometimes?"

"Compared to you, or normal people?"

"Compared to anybody. There's a story here, McGraw. Get it, even if it kills you."

"Heaven forbid," McGraw interjected.

"Whatever. You know, McGraw … politicians have learned to wrap the press around their grimy little fingers. We bend over backwards to be 'fair' and 'objective' and we wind up giving lies the same weight as facts. We print scandal because we're told it sells papers, and then politicians feed the hunger for scandal by flooding us with more rumors, gossip and lies about their opponents. They use terrorist tactics to destroy their opponents, and we become their accomplice because it's good copy. They use fancy rhetoric and propaganda to make it sound like they're going to help the common people, but once in office, they help their rich buddies and stick it to the little guy. And all the time they're telling the little guy it's in his best interest to cut taxes and throw out government programs that help the poor and hungry and protect consumers. And we report it all 'fairly' and 'objectively' without doing anything about it. We put out newspapers that aren't worth the paper they're printed on." Slater slammed a fist against his desk. "Well, that's not good enough! That's not the way it should be! There's still a place for a newspaper that has the guts to dig for the facts." He suddenly realized to whom he was talking. "I'm probably telling this to the wrong reporter, since you've been down in Florida manufacturing stories about Elvis and people with twelve toes, but let's give it a shot."

"Thirteen," McGraw said.

"What?"

"Thirteen toes. We have a rule at the *Exposer*. We don't do stories on people with twelve toes. You've got to have thirteen or it doesn't get in the paper."

"Forget that weird stuff, McGraw. You're back in the big city. And remember … you don't have much time to nail down this story."

Slater ushered McGraw from his office to the State Desk. "Jerome's campaign headquarters is in Springfield, but he's in Peoria, his hometown, for a few speeches today. He'll spend the night there. Get down there and give me a story for tomorrow morning's state edition! Any questions?"

"Just one," McGraw said. "What's the penalty for murdering an editor in this state?"

Cindy Lawson, a copy editor on the state desk, looked up from her computer. "In season or out of season?"

Rob Blake, another copy editor, said, "no penalty. They give you a commendation and a promotion."

"Get back to work!" Slater snarled. He turned to McGraw. "A couple more things. Hold down your expenses! The publisher has ordered us to tighten our belts again. That's like a direct order from God, as far as I'm concerned." He handed McGraw a key and a card. "You'll have the use of a Buick the company leased and this gold credit card, which is in the newspaper's name. You can use it to pay for your room in a cheap hotel, meals when it's absolutely necessary for you to eat, and other essentials. Now get out of here!"

As McGraw wandered toward the exit, exchanging pleasantries with the news crew, Slater called Personnel.

"Amy? Rick Slater. Did you show my personnel file to that sleazebag McGraw? ... Well, how the hell did he find out so much about me? ... Look, personnel records are supposed to be confidential, aren't they? ... Well, you'd better do something to make sure they're kept confidential! If McGraw can get at them, so can any scumbag who walks in off the street!"

McGraw found the black Buick LaCrosse in the *Chronicle* parking deck, stopped by Macy's to buy two more shirts and two pairs of slacks and then returned to the Hyatt Regency, where he threw his clothes and toothbrush into a suitcase.

Minutes later the Buick and McGraw began the three-hour drive to Peoria, where he would confront Harry Jerome. If Jerome was uncooperative, McGraw could put him on the phone with Slater. Sort of a good cop/bad cop thing. Five minutes of listening to Slater would scare the hell out of anyone.

6

McGraw and the Buick cruised south on Interstate 55 that Thursday afternoon. Clouds drifted lazily overhead. Flat prairieland stretched for miles.

McGraw flicked on the car radio. His search for Top Forties music was interrupted when he stumbled upon a Christian station. The Rev. Lawrence Drury, pastor of the First Church of Eternal Life in Springfield, was preaching ...

"... But now our nation's leaders have turned away from God and evil forces are in control. God is not welcome in the White House, in our state capitals, in our schools, or in the minds of men. Everywhere you look, there are signs of decadence and despair. There is no time to waste. The Day of Judgment is coming. We must set the country on the right course by electing to office candidates who are true Christians.

"Harry Jerome, who is running for governor in Illinois, is such a candidate. The Christian Majority for Jerome is raising funds to help put Harry Jerome in the state house. We need your support. Send whatever you have—whether it's five hundred dol-

lars or a measly dollar—because God wants you to help elect Harry Jerome. Call now. The number is 1-800-H JEROME. Operators are waiting for your call."

Twenty miles east of Peoria on Highway 116, McGraw passed a huge photo of Harry Jerome plastered on a billboard. Jerome's smile seemed genuine and his noble facial features commanded respect. Harry looked like the perfect candidate—distinguished, likeable, caring, trustworthy. At a time when image counted for so much, Harry seemed destined to be a winner. "VOTE FOR JEROME — THE FUTURE IS NOW!" the billboard declared.

McGraw headed into Peoria on U.S. 150, which became War Memorial Drive and cut through the heart of the city. It was a scenic route. Cool autumn evenings had turned leaves on maple and oak trees bright red and yellow.

McGraw maneuvered onto Knoxville Avenue and cruised downtown. He discovered Peoria was one of those places where the center city no longer was the place to shop. Instead of large retail stores, the city's downtown housed two hospitals, the world headquarters of Caterpillar, Inc. and a topless joint called Bottomly's.

On Hamilton Street, McGraw caught a glimpse of a storefront bearing a "Jerome for Governor" sign. He parked down the street and returned on foot to check out the small wooden frame building, which looked as though it had once been a retail store. McGraw had expected something more lavish. He suspected the real work on the Jerome campaign took place in Springfield.

A young campaign worker with an infectious smile and the bouncy step of a high school cheerleader greeted McGraw at the entrance. He introduced himself and asked to see Harry Jerome.

"Oh, I'm sorry, but Mr. Jerome isn't in the office," said the girl. She glanced at his schedule of activities during his Peoria visit. "Let's see ... he visited Bradley University's School of Business early this afternoon, then went home to rest. ... Isn't it just tremendous the way he's strangling the opposition?"

McGraw assumed the girl was referring to the latest polls, which showed Jerome nearly even with Governor Dodge. She probably would be a lot of fun at horror movies. She'd be ecstatic when monsters sucked the blood out of their victims.

"Strangling the opposition always gives me goose-bumps," McGraw admitted. "How do I get to Harry's home?"

Jerome's majestic old stone mansion fronted on exclusive Grand View Drive, a winding, scenic, tree-lined road that afforded a stunning view of the Illinois River. A half dozen cars and vans bearing television and radio station call letters were parked nearby. A dozen reporters and cameramen roamed the lawn and driveway, apparently waiting for the candidate to make an appearance.

Fifty feet from the house, McGraw smelled something fragrant, possibly an aromatic bug spray or a pungent perfume. Then he noticed a shapely blonde television reporter wearing a baby blue blouse and dark blue slacks. Positioned so her audience would see Jerome's house looming in the background, she was wrapping up an on-camera report.

"*... It was obvious Harry wasn't going to come out of the house, so I interviewed his gardener. Albert Jones said Harry Jerome is partial to orange roses because Harry's wife, who died in an automobile crash sixteen years ago, loved them. So that's the* *story on Harry Jerome this afternoon. If no news is good news, there's a lot of good news in Peoria today."*

She handed the mike to the tall, chubby cameraman and fluffed her hair. "Did you get that, Wally?"

"Got it," he said. He gathered his equipment. McGraw ducked to avoid being hit as Wally swung it around.

"You have a nice delivery," McGraw told the young woman. "I bet you're terrific when there's something worth reporting."

She smiled. "The station needed a report on Jerome today but there's no news. I considered listing, in reverse order, the top ten reasons why Harry Jerome won't come out to play. You know, like David Letterman does. 'Number Six. Because all his clothes are in the laundry. Number Five. Because he's waiting for his brain to arrive on the next flight from New York.'"

McGraw laughed. "I get the idea."

As he gazed at the vivacious blonde, McGraw realized he must watch his step. She had more curves than Grand View Drive and a warm, seductive smile. She handled herself well. She obviously had been around the block a few times. She was the kind of woman the Old McGraw would have pursued and then, when they finally got together, she would use him and dump him when something better came along. And then the word would get back to Morelli's—probably from McGraw himself, in one of his weaker moments—that he had struck out again and there would be a new round of laughter, and something approaching pity. But those days were over. The New McGraw would avoid short, meaningless relationships and focus instead on long-term liaisons. Women could not use him as their Token Lover any more.

"I'm David McGraw of the *National Exposer*."

He froze. He was mortified. Had he really said that? He wished the earth would open up and swallow him. Or, better yet, her.

"The *National Exposer*?"

She wasn't laughing, but she was on the verge.

"I'm joking. I'm really with the *Chicago Chronicle*."

"I'm Marilyn Westley. I report for Springfield's Channel 10 News. Are you covering Harry's campaign?"

"That's right."

"Well, you'll find that following Harry around the state is about as exciting as watching rain drip off a roof. Most of the time, there isn't much happening. I don't think he likes—or trusts—the press."

"What's with him, anyway?" McGraw asked. "He went to bed early when he won the primary. He avoids the press. He doesn't want to share a platform with Dodge. Two weeks before the election he's cooped up in his house. He's missing a lot of opportunities for free publicity. You wouldn't be able to shut up most politicians. Is Jerome dumb or does he know something nobody else does?"

"Maybe he's not the political animal other politicians are," Marilyn suggested.

"They're all political animals. It's a disease they acquire the moment they decide to run for public office and there's no known cure."

"You're very sure of yourself."

McGraw led her to a shade tree on the lawn. "I've got an editor back in Chicago who's going to have a seizure if I don't file a story about Sleeping Beauty that has some meat to it. What is Jerome really like? Does he go around killing cats, or kicking the homeless? Did he ever run a savings and loan into the ground, or play gin rummy with Fidel Castro?"

Marilyn laughed. "As far as I know, he's a decent human being. He seems nice enough, but I really don't know what he's like. I've only talked to him twice."

McGraw was stunned. "Twice? How long have you been covering the news?"

"Three years. But don't look so surprised. I've only been reporting politics for a month. Jerome stayed out of the limelight before he became a candidate. He ran the Farrell Foundation on the north side of Peoria."

Marilyn liked McGraw's sense of humor. His semi-muscular body had possibilities, too. And he might be half-way intelligent. Certainly he was a step up from the creeps who asked her out. Most of them had wives. Those who didn't had the IQ's of lice. Perhaps McGraw would ask her out. She would give him a hint.

"So how long will you be covering Harry, McGraw?"

"For the duration of the campaign. I'm replacing Carl Yorbly."

"Oh, yes … Too bad about his back. But I won't miss him. Yorbly was a jerk. Kept trying to hit on me. And he was married! If he hadn't been married, he'd still be a jerk! I'm glad you're here instead of Yorbly."

Marilyn wondered if McGraw understood the subtle message she was sending him—that she would be interested in going out with him.

McGraw turned pale. The message he received was that here was a woman who didn't want to be messed with.

McGraw noticed Denny Underwood, a reporter for Martin Hudson's *Chicago Sentinel*, leaning against a van. Underwood had covered the State House when McGraw was covering it for the *Chronicle*. Underwood wasn't much of a reporter, but he was good at picking up press releases and sending them to the *Sentinel*. The older man Underwood was talking to noticed McGraw and hurried over.

"Murray Denton," he said. "Harry Jerome's campaign manager."

McGraw introduced himself.

"You'll want these ..." Denton said, displaying the enthusiasm of a vacuum cleaner salesman. He handed McGraw and Marilyn press packets containing the latest Jerome photos and press releases. "Just let me know if there's anything I can do for you."

"When can I interview Jerome?" McGraw asked. "My boss is expecting a story for tomorrow's paper."

"Sorry. He's resting. No interviews today."

"Sure. Resting," Marilyn muttered. "Screwing up on the campaign trail takes a lot out of a candidate."

"Maybe we're on to something," McGraw said. "Jerome obviously isn't healthy enough to perform the duties of governor. He seems to need a lot of rest and sleep. Is he sick? Is he dying? You know, if he's dying, the public has a right to know about it!"

Denton frowned. "Slow down, pardner. It's nothing like that. Harry's just relaxing a little. All the information you need for a story is in the press packet."

"That's not good enough. I've got to talk to him!"

"And you will, McGraw. But not today."

Denton hurried off as McGraw thumbed through the press packet. Not much there except an outline of Jerome's views on the issues, a fistful of speeches, details about his background and five photos.

McGraw skimmed the background sheet. Harry Ashley Jerome was born to a middle class family in Ukiah, California, and was raised there. Played football at San Jose State University in San Jose, California, graduating in 1977. Married his childhood sweetheart, Nancy Williams, the same year. Served in Vietnam, winning a medal for heroism. Opened an insurance agency in 1981. In 1996, when the Jeromes were vacationing in West Germany, Nancy Jerome was killed in an automobile crash on an autobahn near West Berlin. Two years later, Jerome moved to Peoria and joined the staff of the Farrell Foundation. Over the next fourteen years, he managed the Farrell Foundation and served on the boards of several institutions and manufacturing companies, including the Madden Collector Card Company, the Lincoln Road State Bank of Illinois and Sue Ellen Jerrell Enterprises. Photos showed Harry playing football, wearing a military uniform, working at the Farrell Foundation, saving the life of the convenience store clerk and campaigning for governor.

McGraw realized that uncovering the real Harry Jerome was not going to be easy. Denton seemed determined to control the flow of information.

McGraw glanced at his watch. It was a few minutes after five. He needed to check in with Slater. "Nice meeting you, Marilyn," he said, as he hustled back to the Buick.

"Same to you, McGraw."

McGraw climbed into the Buick and dialed Slater on his cell phone. He told Slater the press packet contained only superficial biographical information about Harry Jerome and he would not be permitted to interview Jerome until the candidate finished "resting".

"You can't even talk to Jerome?" Slater roared. "This isn't going to look good on your resume, McGraw—'fired because he couldn't find the candidate for governor he was assigned to cover.' I didn't send you down there for a vacation, McGraw. Your career is in my hands and if it gets smashed to smithereens, I wouldn't lose any sleep. *Get me the story, McGraw!*"

McGraw drove back downtown, as he pondered his next move. The more he thought, the angrier he got. Here was a man running for governor of Illinois and he couldn't even catch a glimpse of him. Nobody was going to get away with that. McGraw would show that slimeball Slater what real reporting was. If Harry Ashley Jerome had something to hide, McGraw would find out what it was.

7

McGraw treated himself to a prime rib dinner at Bennigan's Grill and Tavern in the Holiday Inn, paying for it with the *Chronicle* credit card. Afterward, he hiked through quiet, darkened streets to the Public Library on Monroe Street.

At the information desk, he asked to see recent issues of the *Peoria Reporter*. He was directed to an area on the first floor packed with microfilm-viewing machines.

As McGraw browsed pages of the *Reporter* from early summer, he became vaguely aware someone had pulled up a chair beside him. It was Marilyn, wearing a black leather jacket and tight-fitting black slacks.

"What are you doing here?" McGraw asked.

"I saw you go into the library and figured I'd see what a big city reporter does when he can't get a story. I notice you're stealing material from Harry's hometown paper."

"Not at all. I'm looking for background information. In the big city, we call this 'research'. It's a concept you downstate cub reporters might not be familiar with."

McGraw turned the crank and advanced the microfilm several pages. He was reading about Jerome's pledge to lower business taxes when he realized Marilyn was still a few feet away, staring at him.

"You really don't have anything better to do, do you?" he asked.

Marilyn blushed. "I had a date tonight, but I canceled. I've been going out too much."

"Probably bar-hopping trying to pick up men."

Marilyn bristled. "I'm not that kind of woman, McGraw."

Not that kind of woman? Who was she kidding? She was slick and sophisticated. And she didn't learn to dress in leather jackets and tight leather slacks by hanging around convents. She was that kind of woman, all right ... the kind who would lure McGraw into her web, then spit him out when she was done with him.

"Who was your date with?"

"Denny Underwood. The *Chicago Sentinel* reporter."

"I know Denny. ... Didn't realize he was dating."

"Why not?"

McGraw turned his attention back to the microfilm. "He's married."

Marilyn choked. *That* took her by surprise.

"Water fountain's over there," McGraw said, nodding to a far corner of the room.

She swallowed some water and returned.

"Actually, it wasn't a date. We planned to compare notes on Jerome. Things like that."

McGraw skimmed two more stories about Jerome. "Denton's running a slick and professional campaign," McGraw observed. "Jerome says all the right things—except for occasional screwups when he ad-libs. He belittles Governor

Dodge at the same time he claims he's taking the 'higher ground'. He seems likeable enough, but there's no meat in these stories—only fluff, empty rhetoric and propaganda."

McGraw advanced the microfilm and noticed a short interview with the head of the Farrell Foundation.

Farrell Foundation CEO Lauds Jerome For Entering Race

Harry Jerome will make a great governor, according to Richard Dunnington, head of Peoria's Farrell Foundation.

Jerome served as president of the foundation before announcing his candidacy in January.

"I've never met anyone else who was so eminently qualified for a position of leadership," Dunnington said. "Jerome did a terrific job running the foundation, and he'll do a tremendous job running the state.

"I remember the day Harry started work at the foundation twelve years ago. He was as full of energy and enthusiasm as he is today. Harry has always done everything he possibly could for the foundation and the community. He will make an outstanding governor!"

"Look at that," McGraw remarked. "Dunnington says he remembers the day Harry started work at the foundation twelve years ago, but Denton's press release says Harry came to the foundation fourteen years ago."

"Probably an honest mistake."

"Maybe, but all of these news reports are vague about Jerome's years at the foundation. What did he do there? What kind of work does the foundation do? Is foundation money behind his candidacy?"

"One thing is sure," Marilyn said. "Everything about Jerome and his campaign is totally controlled. Nothing is left to chance. The vagueness is obviously part of their campaign strategy. They figure the more they control what the public knows about Jerome, the better his chances of being elected."

McGraw shook his head. "Why haven't you and Underwood and the other reporters been doing your jobs? You accept Jerome handouts like lap dogs. You haven't done any digging to find out what Jerome really stands for. Nobody knows anything about him."

"I suppose it's easier to accept the handouts they give us without question. But the *Chronicle* is to blame, too. Carl Yorbly was as complacent as the rest of us."

"Face it, Westley. You weren't doing your job! Quit trying to pass the blame."

"Why you egotistical jerk. You come in here—one day on the job—and you can't even find Harry. Who are *you* to criticize *me*?"

"I guess it's up to me to do the job you and the other reporters should have been doing. I'll find out what's really going on!"

"Lots of luck, McGraw. He won't even talk to you."

"That's the difference between you and me. I'm an investigative reporter. I won't stop until I've got the story. You're a gofer at a piddling little radio station."

"*Television station, McGraw! It's a television station! Get your facts straight! ...* Just because you work for a Chicago paper, you think you're God's gift to journalism." She looked at him slyly. "By the way … did you ever work for the *National Exposer*?"

McGraw shifted uneasily in his chair. "What? Are you crazy? Do you think I'd work for a rag like that?"

"You didn't answer my question. You mentioned the *Exposer* earlier today. There must have been a reason. Did you work for the *Exposer*?"

"Define 'work' …"

"Did they employ you? Did they pay you a salary?"

He grimaced. "I was at the *Exposer* for a few months. It was during a period in my life when I thought I'd enjoy making big bucks and living in Florida."

"How long ago was that 'period in your life'?"

"Yesterday morning."

"Let me get this straight. You're lording it over the rest of us who are covering Jerome, telling us what jerks we are, but you cut your journalistic teeth at the *National Exposer*."

"I reported for the *Chronicle* five years before I joined the *Exposer*. And I was a damn good reporter. I know what I'm talking about. Yes, I worked at the *Exposer*, but I didn't let it corrupt my integrity as a journalist."

"That's like saying you spent the night in a whorehouse but you didn't take off your pants."

"I was an innocent in the land of the Sirens, a mere spectator to the carnage inside the carnival tent. Besides, I was only doing it for the money."

"There's a definition of a prostitute if I ever heard one," Marilyn noted.

McGraw advanced the microfilm. "Well, whatever I do about Harry, it will be out of your league. Go back to your little fifty-watt TV station and tell them in sixteen different ways that the candidate won't talk to you. Meantime, I'll be finding out what makes Jerome tick."

Marilyn rose out of her chair. "McGraw, I've had it with your holier-than-thou attitude. You might as well go back to Chicago because you won't get anywhere with Jerome. I'll nail down this story before you find your way out of the library ... and you can quote me in the *National Exposer*!"

McGraw chuckled. "The *Exposer* wouldn't quote you unless you had three breasts under that jacket or five bodies in your apartment."

Marilyn stomped off, hips swaying provocatively from side-to-side. Too bad she had such an abrasive personality, McGraw thought. She would be dynamite in bed if she could transform all that verbal abuse into sexual energy.

8

After a fitful night of tossing and turning at the Hotel Pere Marquette, McGraw sampled the breakfast specialties in the hotel's American Cafe, paying for it with the *Chronicle* credit card. Then he drove to the north side of Peoria where, after a few wrong turns, he stumbled upon the Farrell Foundation. He figured someone at the foundation would be able to tell him more about Harry Jerome and the institution the candidate headed for twelve—or fourteen—years.

The foundation was housed in a modern, one-story granite building on Allen Road. McGraw parked the Buick between two BMWs and head-to-head with a Cadillac. The foundation obviously was not the type of place where public aid recipients hung out.

Overwhelming silence in the lobby reminded McGraw of the somber mood inside a funeral home. When a prim, middle-aged brunette at the reception desk asked if she could help him, McGraw found himself whispering.

"I'd like to see Harry Jerome." It was worth a try.

"I'm so sorry, but since he became a candidate, Mr. Jerome no longer comes to the foundation."

"Perhaps someone else could talk to me about Mr. Jerome and his work at the foundation. I'm a reporter for the *Chicago Chronicle*."

The receptionist—whose nameplate identified her as Esther Pritchard—asked McGraw to be seated while she inquired. A few moments later, Ms. Pritchard informed McGraw that someone would talk with him shortly.

Minutes later, a black-haired, middle-aged, slightly nervous man dressed like an undertaker approached the reception area. "I'm Richard Dunnington, chairman of the board. How may I help you?"

"David McGraw, *Chicago Chronicle*. I'd like to talk to you about Harry Jerome."

Dunnington suggested McGraw come back to his office and led the way down a long hallway. The carpet was a golden shag, the walls a cream color. On one office door appeared the name Harry Jerome, chiseled in gold leaf. The door was closed.

In his office, Dunnington motioned for McGraw to be seated in a brown high-back Italian leather chair. Light brown drapes and carpeting complemented cream-colored walls. A print on the wall depicted a matador stabbing a bull. That's probably what the foundation does to pesky reporters, McGraw thought.

"You must know Jerome well," McGraw suggested.

"Certainly. Harry came to the foundation twelve years ago. It was immediately obvious that Harry had exceptional administrative abilities and after two years, the board unanimously elected him president of the foundation."

"Are you sure it was twelve years ago?"

"Yes, of course."

"I see. The press packet that Murray Denton gave me noted that Jerome came to the foundation two years after his wife died in a car crash. That would have been fourteen years ago."

Dunnington smiled. "Well, I'm sure Mr. Denton is right. I didn't have the exact dates in front of me. I should be more careful."

"What type of work did Mr. Jerome do at the foundation?"

Dunnington leaned back in his chair. "He handled administrative matters—the budgeting, the consideration of applications from those seeking grants from the foundation, speeches on foundation policies. Why, Harry could handle just about anything required of him."

"Exactly what does the foundation do?"

Dunnington sighed. "I don't have time to go into detail, but let me give you the fifty-cent version. The Farrell Foundation was established by Wilferd Hayes Farrell, a Peoria industrialist who made a fortune manufacturing bicycles before automobiles arrived on the scene. Mr. Farrell decided he could use his wealth to help those who support the American Way of Life. We award grants to writers who explain the merits of a free economy, fund public television projects that encourage the pursuit of individual freedom, give financial support to publications we deem deserving of our support ... that sort of thing. We also publish our own magazine, *The Farrell Report*."

Dunnington handed a copy of the magazine to McGraw, who skimmed the headlines on the cover:

**The Liberal Plot to
Subvert Our Schools**

LET THEM KEEP THEIR BILLIONS!
***Taxing the Wealthy
Won't Create Jobs***

**Fifty Books That
Should Be Banned**

**THE LIBERAL CONSPIRACY
TO CURTAIL YOUR FREEDOM**

Real Men Carry Guns

"Have you been outside the doors of the foundation lately?" McGraw asked. "The real world might surprise you."

Dunnington patted the cover of *The Farrell Report*. "This *is* the real world, Mr. McGraw."

"Good Lord ... where have I been?"

"Beg your pardon?"

"Uh, nothing ... Is any foundation money supporting Jerome's campaign?"

"No, though some foundation executives have made personal contributions. I have, for one."

"I see. Did Jerome remarry after his wife's death?"

"No, he didn't. He was so totally devastated. He immersed himself in work."

"I'm trying to look behind the image and find out what kind of man Harry Jerome really is. What does he do to relax? Does he go to baseball games, or collect guns, or go bowling? Does he throw dinner parties for Nazis? Has he ever maimed or murdered anyone?"

The ringing of Dunnington's telephone interrupted McGraw. Dunnington uttered a few words into the receiver, then told McGraw he was sorry, but he did not have any more time to talk. "Perhaps some photos of Harry would help," Dunnington suggested.

That would be a start, McGraw agreed. Dunnington pulled a half dozen photos out of a drawer and handed them to McGraw, who was crestfallen to see they were the same photos Murray Denton already had passed out.

On his way down the long hallway that led back to the reception area, McGraw opened the door to Harry Jerome's office and snuck inside. There wasn't much to suggest Jerome had ever worked there. A few bulky volumes on the bookshelves dealt with foundation grants and administration. An unused appointment book lay open on the oak desk. Inside the desk drawers were a two-year-old telephone book, a ream of paper, and a dog-eared copy of *Forbes* magazine that listed the forty richest car dealers in America.

McGraw left the foundation feeling more frustrated than ever. Harry Jerome remained a shadowy figure, shaped only by hype and press releases. Why was it so difficult to find out what Harry was really like?

9

McGraw drove back to Jerome's house on Grandview Drive, arriving as the reporters camped out there were leaving.

"Did you oversleep, McGraw?" Marilyn asked.

"I've been working. Where is everyone going?"

She showed him the news release Press Secretary Duncan Jamieson had just handed out:

> CONFIDENT JEROME TO RELAX
> BEFORE FINAL PUSH FOR VOTES
>
> Harry Jerome, the Independent Alliance Party's candidate for governor, is taking a day off from the rigors of campaigning to relax and review campaign strategy.
>
> "We are on the threshold of victory!" Jerome proclaimed at a thousand-dollar-a-plate fundraiser in Peoria last night. "Tell Governor Dodge to pack his bags and start reading the help wanted ads because a new and glorious day is dawning in Illinois!"

> Jerome will begin a final push for votes on Saturday with a campaign swing through downstate Illinois.

"This guy is certifiable," McGraw grumbled. "No candidate in his right mind would take time off from the campaign now, when ten days remain before the election. It doesn't add up. Slater isn't going to like this."

"Who's Slater?" Marilyn asked.

"My boss. The *Chronicle* state editor. You've probably seen him in a late night horror flick on cable teevee. The only way to stop him is to drive a '54 Buick through his heart."

A bearded man wearing earrings and a Eulenco insignia on his jacket approached them. He seemed to be about thirty years old.

"Isn't this the biggest crock you've ever seen?" he said, waving a copy of the press release.

McGraw and Marilyn looked at each other in surprise.

"It sure is," McGraw said. "But are you supposed to say that? Don't you work for Eulenco?"

"Eulenco owns my body eight hours a day. Twelve when the going gets rough. I own my soul. Or what's left of it."

The reporters introduced themselves. The bearded man did not offer to identify himself.

"What do you know about this?" McGraw asked. "Why would a candidate take a day off during the most crucial phase of the campaign?"

The bearded man glanced furtively around the premises, then whispered, "This is off the record. They try to keep us flunkies in the dark about campaign strategy, but from what I hear, the big cheeses behind the campaign are scared stiff.

Jerome is moving up in the polls, but he's showing signs of coming down with Foot-in-Mouth Disease. The power brokers can't afford any more blunders. They're going to coach Jerome, try to pull him through the last days of the campaign without blowing the whole thing."

McGraw knew Marilyn was thinking the same thing he was—it was a good story. But since it was off the record, he couldn't write anything about it unless he got it from another source.

The long hair shrugged. "Look, I've said too much already. I've got to go."

"Wait!" Marilyn implored. "What's your name?"

"It's not important."

As McGraw returned to the Buick, Marilyn followed at a distance. She stealthily approached McGraw from behind as he dialed a number on his cell phone. He didn't notice Marilyn because he was preoccupied with ogling a blonde in a red DeVille. Marilyn could hear McGraw's end of the conversation ...

"Tell Slater his favorite reporter is calling from Peoria."

McGraw could hear the assistant editor hollering to Slater "your buddy McGraw is on the line".

"Why are you calling, McGraw?" Slater growled. "I don't want to talk to you, I want you to file stories. It's a simple system, but it works for us."

"There's a problem. Bashful Harry is still hiding out. I did find out that his blunders are panicking his handlers, but I haven't got that from a source I can use."

"You didn't talk to Jerome?"

"I couldn't, Slater. The guy is holed up in his house."

"What the hell have you been doing the last two days?" Slater roared.

"Trying to interview Jerome. It's impossible. Nobody has seen him!"

Slater heard a familiar voice on a television set in the *Chronicle* newsroom and turned to see Jerome on the screen. "Well, somebody has seen him!" Slater snarled. He held the telephone close to the television. A reporter was saying the video footage, supplied by the Jerome campaign, showed the candidate visiting a nursing home in Peoria. The reporter noted that Jerome hugged several residents and assured them he would champion their cause when he became governor.

Slater got back on the line. "So where the hell were you when Jerome visited the old folks, McGraw?"

"I have no idea. It doesn't make sense. His advisors wouldn't let any reporters close to him. He was resting."

"Face it, McGraw. You've been goofing off. This assignment may be too much for you. ... I'll give you one last chance. Talking to Harry won't give you everything you need, anyway. It'll take leg work. Get off your ass and fly out to California this weekend. Get the *Chronicle* an exclusive on Jerome and what makes him tick! Visit the town where he grew up. Find out what he was like years ago. Find out why he ducks the press. Is he a reclusive jackass or is he hiding something? ... But I'm warning you, McGraw. If you fail again, don't bother returning to the *Chronicle*!"

"All right. I'll hitch a plane to California this afternoon. But, Slater, a little advice: reporters work better when they're not threatened. When I run the State Desk, things will be different. ... Hello? ... Slater, are you there?"

Slater had hung up. Obviously, he couldn't take constructive criticism.

As McGraw paused for a few moments to mull things over, Marilyn scurried back to her car.

McGraw returned to the Hotel Pere Marquette, where he called Jerome's campaign headquarters.

Murray Denton had dropped by campaign headquarters after he and Jamieson created the press release about Jerome's day off. Helluva way to run a campaign.

Denton flipped through a stack of telephone messages and noticed Richard Dunnington had called. When Denton returned the foundation president's call, Dunnington informed him McGraw had visited the foundation in search of information about Jerome. Denton's conversation with Dunnington was interrupted when the bouncy, cheerleader-type, horror-movie-loving office girl informed Denton someone on another line had asked to speak to him.

"Denton here."

"McGraw here."

"Of course, McGraw. *Chicago Chronicle*, right? ... What can I do for you?"

"I hear Jerome isn't taking a breather because he's confident and relaxed. It's because some of your people are terrified Harry is losing it, screwing up on the campaign trail and ruining his chances of winning."

"Not true, McGraw! I emphatically deny that. Don't deal in rumors. If you want facts, come to me."

"Okay. I want to interview Jerome today."

"Sorry. No can do."

"I'm tired of playing patty-cake with you and Jerome. I'm flying out to California this afternoon to dig into Harry's past. He was raised in Ukiah and attended San Jose State. Is that right?"

Denton seemed rattled. "That's right, McGraw, but there's nothing there. You'd be wasting your time. If you need information, I can get it for you."

"Okay. What is Jerome's private phone number?"

"Can't help you."

"Haven't got time to tap dance with you. Got a plane to catch. Goodbye, Murray."

Denton phoned Roger Moss in Springfield.

"I hope Randall has contained the situation out west because we've got another problem. David McGraw of the *Chicago Chronicle* is flying to California to snoop around."

"San Jose's no problem," Moss said, "and Randall is mopping up in Ukiah. I'll have Wolfman tail McGraw every step of the way. If McGraw finds anything, we'll take care of it."

"Don't get carried away. If you kill a reporter, we'll be in more trouble than you can imagine!"

"You worry too much, Denton. Do your job. I'll do mine."

McGraw checked out of the Pere Marquette and drove to the Greater Peoria Regional Airport. After parking the Buick in the long-term lot, he purchased a round-trip ticket to San Francisco. He had always wanted to see the Bay Area. Now, thanks to the elusive Harry Jerome, he would be able to.

III

California Manhunt

10

Friday afternoon McGraw boarded a United Express flight bound for Chicago. After a short wait at O'Hare International Airport, he settled into a United jet that would take him to the San Francisco Bay area.

As the jet skimmed the clouds over Iowa, McGraw tried to relax. Suddenly his newspaper career—which had looked so promising when he flew out of Florida—showed signs of self-destructing. What would he do if he lost his job? He had no intention of slinging hamburgers at Burger King, or laying pipe in Alaska, or moving to his parents' home in Wisconsin. Of course, he could return to Florida and shovel gossip and sleaze at the *National Exposer* until the end of time, but that was a little like going back to the loony bin after you had been released.

McGraw opened his laptop computer. He should file some sort of story for Slater. He would write about the difficulty he was having tracking down the elusive Harry Jerome. A story like that might pressure Murray Denton into setting up an interview with Jerome. McGraw began typing...

From: McGraw
Attn: Slater, supreme ruler of the State Desk

HARRY & ME

Why is gubernatorial candidate Harry
Jerome hiding from the press and the
public?

Reporters usually don't have much difficulty arranging interviews with candidates for
public office. It's generally hard to shut them
up unless you put muzzles on them and throw
them over a cliff. Thus, it came as a surprise
to this newsman when he could not even get
near Harry Jerome. What is going on?

Murray Denton, Jerome's campaign
manager, insists Jerome isn't hiding. ...

A strangely familiar female voice interrupted McGraw's
concentration. The voice was talking to the middle-aged
businessman seated next to McGraw. "This man is subject
to violent seizures," the voice was saying. "I'm his nurse.
Would you mind if I switched seats with you? He usually
doesn't hurt anyone, but there was an unfortunate incident
in Dallas when he attempted to strangle an FBI agent."

McGraw cringed. When he looked up, Marilyn was settling into the seat beside him. "I also strangle smartass television reporters. What are you doing here? Have you been
following me since I left Peoria?"

"Well, I happened to overhear your conversation with
your boss this morning ..."

"Happened to overhear it? I was a block away from
where I left you!"

"Let's not quibble over details. Anyway, I talked the station into letting me go to California with you!"

"What? Who invited you? You're nothing but trouble! My life was moving along pretty well until I met you."

"Now, McGraw, I know it's difficult, but try to think rationally. Two professionals stand a better chance of tracking down the information we need. We can cover all the ground we need to cover in California in half the time. It's perfect. What do you say?"

He nodded toward an "exit" sign. "You want to jump, or should I?"

"We'll make a great team, McGraw! You can get a lot more done with me along!"

McGraw sighed. There was a certain logic to her reasoning. "All right. Since you're here and I can't seem to get rid of you, we'll try it."

"Good. Uh, there is one problem ... I work for a small television station, McGraw. We wouldn't send a reporter out of state to cover a story if a 'quake destroyed half the country. The station manager said I could fly to California, but he won't pay my expenses. ... You know that gold credit card you used to buy your ticket back in Peoria ..."

"What? You expect my newspaper to pay your expenses?"

"We'll be working together ... sharing information. I'll be helping the *Chronicle*."

McGraw gritted his teeth. "You've got a lot of guts, Marilyn. Not many brains, but a lot of guts. Maybe there's something else I could do for you, like buying you a house by the lake."

"No, this will be quite enough, thank you."

She examined the text on McGraw's laptop.

"That's cute. 'Harry & Me'. Like the movie 'Roger & Me',

where that guy went looking for the big honcho at General Motors but couldn't get near him. Very good, McGraw!"

"Would you pipe down so I can work?"

He struggled with his story a few minutes longer. Then Marilyn interrupted again.

"We ought to plan what we'll do after we land in San Francisco," she suggested.

"I intend to check into a hotel for a good night's sleep and try to forget I ever met you and Slater."

"My, aren't we grumpy," Marilyn said, smiling. "Did we get up on the wrong side of the garbage dump this morning?"

"I don't know if we did, but I did. You're destroying my career!"

"Oh, is that all."

McGraw tried to calm down. "All right. We'll rent cars at the airport. Saturday morning, you can drive to San Jose. See if you can find anything on the San Jose State campus that sheds light on Jerome's past. I'll drive to Ukiah and see what I can find out about the years he spent there."

"Fair enough," Marilyn said.

McGraw continued working on "Harry & Me". A half hour later he shut down the computer, leaned back, closed his eyes and slipped into a relaxing nap.

When McGraw awoke, the jet was sweeping over a mountain range and a flight attendant was serving prepackaged steak-and-potato dinners.

McGraw glanced around the plane. Most of the travelers seemed fairly normal, but a scruffy-looking, long-haired guy in an army jacket four rows behind McGraw was a puzzle. His steel-blue eyes seemed to pierce right through McGraw.

A half hour later, as the jet swooped down to land at San Francisco International Airport, rays of the setting sun passed through a smattering of clouds, creating a dazzling pink and blue sky over San Francisco Bay.

"Isn't it beautiful, McGraw!" Marilyn exclaimed. "Isn't it gorgeous!"

McGraw, the worldly supermarket tabloid veteran, shrugged. Once you've dwelled in the realm of UFO sightings and reincarnations, it takes more than a good-looking sunset to knock you off your feet.

Inside the terminal, McGraw rented two cars and arranged for them to be dropped off at their hotel the next morning. Then the two reporters rode a shuttle to the Bay Vista Hotel in San Mateo, about ten minutes away.

The Bay Vista was a sprawling, five-story high Mediterranean-style hotel with a heated outdoor pool surrounded by tables and a snack bar called Crazy Louie's. The lobby had a high ceiling and off to the side were the Vista Grill and several small shops.

The young man working the desk wore a tag that identified him as Trent. He checked his computer and informed McGraw that his room on the third floor was ready.

Trent turned his attention to Marilyn. "And you are ..."

"Without a reservation."

Trent smiled. "Let's see what we can do about that."

He gave Marilyn a form to fill out. Five minutes later she had a room on the second floor.

After settling into their rooms and washing up, Marilyn joined McGraw in the Vista Grill for dinner. As they waited for their pork chops and steaks, Marilyn said, "McGraw, sum up your perspective on dating in one headline."

He swirled his beer and thought about that. "FIRE DESTROYS CHARITY—NO SURVIVORS."

"Meaning what?"

"I enter relationships with high hopes. And I always get burned. Seems like I give out a lot and get nothing back. I'm trying to turn over a new leaf because I'm tired of being used, abused and excused by shallow, self-centered women. I'm going to hold out for something better. ... When you came along, I knew I had to watch my step because you're the kind of woman the Old McGraw would have been nuts about."

"Shallow and self-centered?"

"No. Attractive and sophisticated. Only later would I find out you're shallow and self-centered."

"Am I being complimented or insulted?"

"Nothing personal. It's just the way this stupid dating game works."

"I have the same problem."

"You've been dating shallow women?"

"No. Shallow, self-centered men. It isn't worth the aggravation."

"Exactly. ... What would your headline be?"

"ILLINOIS WOMAN FOUND IN LOVE NEST WITH TRENT."

"The desk clerk? You're hopeless."

"I'm kidding, McGraw. Let me think a minute. ... I've got it. 'ABUSED WOMAN VOWS REVENGE'."

"You have some unresolved issues, don't you. ... I knew I had to be careful around you that first night at the library, when you wore tight leather slacks and told me you had a date with a married man. This woman is trouble, I told myself."

"But, McGraw. Like I told you. I'm not that kind of woman. I'm a good girl who's met a lot of bad and stupid men."

"Which kind I am?"

"The jury's still out on that one."

"So, it sounds to me like we've both been burned and we're both looking for something better. It would be a big mistake for us to get involved. We just happen to be here ... in San Mateo ... at the same hotel ... I think I'd better change hotels."

"Nonsense. We're both adults. We've recognized our mistakes and we can learn from them."

"Right."

Marilyn finished off her beer. "I'm going to sit by the pool. See you tomorrow."

McGraw retired to his room, kicked off his loafers and used the hotel's Internet connection to surf the Net, looking for information about Ukiah, California ...

City of about 15,000 people, county seat of Mendocino County. He checked a realty site and was amazed at the cost of buying a home in Ukiah. Small one or two bedrooms that would go for about seventy or eighty grand in central Illinois were listed at $275,000 or $300,000 — or more.

McGraw watched a little television. After the late local news ended, he was brushing his teeth when someone knocked on the door connecting his room to the suite next to it. Marilyn, looking ravishing in a revealing pink negligee, informed McGraw that because her room on the second floor did not have hot water, she had been reassigned to the room next to his on the third floor.

"What time do you want to meet for breakfast in the morning?" she asked.

"Uh ...What?" He was still looking at her negligee.

"What time for breakfast?"

"Oh. Seven-thirty."

"See you then," she said, turning to leave.

"Uh ... Say, Marilyn. Would you like to stay ..."

But the door shut and Marilyn was on the other side.

McGraw turned out his light and endured a restless night of tossing and turning.

Wolfman called Moss from the hotel.

"There are two of them."

"Two what?"

"McGraw and a chick. She flew out here with him. Registered as Marilyn Westley."

"Crap. She's a reporter, too! ... Try to find out where they're going. If they go to Ukiah, don't worry about it. Randall's there and we've got it covered. If they go somewhere else, follow them!"

11

By the time they rendezvoused in the hotel coffee shop the next morning for pancakes and sausage, McGraw had brushed aside thoughts of a romantic liaison with Marilyn. There was no time for distractions. If he didn't find out what Jerome was up to, he wouldn't be reporting for newspapers—he'd be delivering them in a battered station wagon at four in the morning.

Wolfman slipped into the booth next to theirs but kept his back to them. The two reporters were wrestling with maps. Marilyn was trying to figure out how to drive to the San Jose State University campus. McGraw was checking the best way to drive to Ukiah. Wolfman knew Moss would want him to follow Marilyn.

After breakfast, McGraw used the *Chronicle* credit card to withdraw cash. McGraw then reluctantly handed the card over to Marilyn to use for her expenses.

Their rental cars had been driven to the hotel. McGraw's was a red Saturn, Marilyn's a blue Camaro. "I'll meet you back here for dinner," McGraw hollered, as he drove away.

As McGraw started the trek to Ukiah, Marilyn drove around the bustling Bay to San Jose. Wolfman—driving a rented Jeep— stayed close behind.

Nestled in Silicon Valley, the home of many computer hardware and software companies, San Jose was the state's third largest city, with a population of more than a million people. In the heart of the city was San Jose State University and its nearly 30,000 students and 1,600 faculty members. The sprawling campus undoubtedly had changed considerably since Jerome attended the school. Even so, Marilyn thought, it might be the place to begin tearing holes in the shroud of mystery surrounding Harry Jerome. College years often are formative years for a young man. What type of person was Jerome when he was an undergraduate? Finding someone who actually knew Jerome when he was a student was a longshot, but she might find nuggets of information about him in back issues of the college newspaper.

Marilyn followed signs to the campus and guided the Camaro into a visitors' parking lot. Dozens of students in sweatshirts, jackets and jeans hiked across campus at a leisurely pace.

Marilyn asked a coed for directions to the campus newspaper offices. The coed pointed in the direction of a small concrete building. "Newspaper," she said.

"Are you on drugs?" Marilyn asked.

The coed shook her head. "Only novocaine. Came from dentist."

A few minutes later, Marilyn entered the crowded and noisy newsroom of the *Spartan Times*. Angie, a sophomore with light brown hair, led her to the small room which housed old copies of the *Spartan Times* and files of clippings from the *Times*.

"We're trying to put everything on the computer," Angie said. "It'll probably take us, oh, twenty or thirty years."

Marilyn discovered several sports stories about Harry Jerome, highly regarded halfback on the 1975 and 1976 Spartan football teams, and a half dozen photos of him. The gutsy young athlete bore a certain resemblance to the Harry Jerome of thirty years later. Other articles revealed Jerome was vice president of his senior class, a starter on the Spartan baseball team, an honor student, and editor of a student literary magazine.

Marilyn make copies of the articles and photos on the office copier.

"Do you suppose there's anyone around campus who knew Harry when he was a student?" Marilyn asked.

"The football coach has only been here ten years and the athletic director not much longer. Try Professor Blakely. He's been around here so long some people say they built the campus around him. He teaches English."

"Where could I find him today?"

"Let's see if he teaches any Saturday classes."

Angie accessed a class schedule on a computer. "He does have a creative writing class later this morning. He might be over at the Faculty Office Building now."

Angie took her outside and showed her the way to the large Spartan Complex, which housed sports facilities, and the Faculty Office Building just north of it where Blakely's office was located.

As Marilyn crossed the campus, she thought for a moment someone was watching her from behind a parked Jeep. It might have been the steely-eyed, army-jacketed tough guy McGraw had pointed out on the plane, but when Marilyn looked again, no one was there. She concluded her eyes were playing tricks on him.

On the first floor of the Faculty Office Building, Marilyn stumbled upon the office of Professor Elton Blakely. She knocked and was relieved when a voice told her to enter.

"Professor Blakely?"

"Yes."

A short, thin, gray-haired man, Blakely wore a light brown suit, a rumpled white shirt and a stained yellow tie. He seemed to be in his sixties. The professor studied Marilyn carefully, evidently trying to remember if Marilyn was one of his students, past or present.

After Marilyn introduced herself, Blakely asked her to sit in a wooden, straight-backed chair. Bookshelves stuffed with novels and poetry lined the walls of the small office. Student compositions cluttered the desk.

"How can I help you, Miss Westley?"

"Do you remember a student named Harry Jerome? He attended classes here in the 1970s."

Blakely leaned back in his chair and scratched his head. "Jerome … Harry Jerome …"

"Harry Ashley Jerome, if that's of any help."

Blakely sighed. "There have been so many students. The years all seem to run together."

"Brown hair," Marilyn continued. "Probably a political science major. He played football."

"Football … oh, yes! … I do remember him, I think. Capable young man. No Dostoyevsky, but he wrote pretty fair compositions."

"Harry wants to be the next governor of Illinois."

"Really! How wonderful."

"He has the image of being an All-American, small-town-and-apple-pie type of youngster. Did he seem at all strange or reclusive when you knew him?"

Blakely smiled. For a few moments, he seemed to be back in the early Sixties. "Strange or reclusive? No, quite the contrary. Very normal. Popular. Easy-going."

"As a candidate, Harry has been hiding from the press and his appearances have been carefully controlled. I haven't been able to interview him."

"Well, people change, Miss Westley. Perhaps Harry decided that was the way to win the election."

"Did you hear any more about Harry after he left here?"

"Not until years later, when his son was in my class."

"*His son?* I didn't know he had one."

"Oh, yes. I recall Harry came to see me once when he visited Harry Junior on campus. Harry seemed happy with his life."

"That must have been shortly before his wife died in an automobile accident in Germany."

"My goodness. I had no idea. How sad."

"Did he have any other children?"

"I really don't know."

"Did you hear from Harry or his son after Harry Junior left school?"

"No, not a word. I wouldn't be surprised if Harry Junior's son shows up on campus one day, but I'll probably be gone by then."

After Marilyn left Professor Blakely's office, Wolfman slipped in.

"My sister was just here. Did she say where she was going?"

Blakely, who looked forward to quiet Saturdays on campus, was not pleased to be facing another uninvited guest. "No. That was your sister?"

"That's right. Were you able to tell her anything about Harry Jerome?"

"Not much. Guess she didn't know he had a son."

"No, I suppose not. Anything else?"

"No."

"Thanks, pops."

As Wolfman left the building, he spotted Marilyn in the distance and followed her as he called Moss on his cell phone.

"The girl knows Jerome had a son. One of the professors told her."

"This boat is springing more leaks than the Titanic," Moss grumbled. "Stay on her, Wolfman. I've gotta call Randall in Ukiah."

As Marilyn hurried across campus, she pondered her next move. Should she keep the revelation that Harry had a son to herself, or should she share it with that egocentric Chicago reporter? The pleasure she would derive from using the information first and then rubbing McGraw's face in it would be sublime, but she had made a pact to share information, and she was the one who had proposed the pact. Reluctantly, she concluded she had no choice but to tell McGraw about Harry Junior. Having a conscience could be a real pain at times.

She picked up her cell phone and dialed ...

12

As McGraw's Saturn sped along U.S. 101 about seventy miles north of San Francisco his cell phone rang.

"McGraw."

"It's Marilyn. I—"

"Marilyn! I was just thinking about you."

"You were?"

"Yeah. I noticed that the further I get away from you, the more well-adjusted and saner I am. It's an inverse relationship!"

"Cute, McGraw, but not true. You could drive a thousand miles and you'd still be crazy as a loon."

"Why are you calling? Don't you know it's illegal to use a cell phone while driving in California?"

"I'm not driving."

"I am. ... Oh, I get it. You figure if you get me arrested, you can steal the story."

"Grow up, McGraw. I don't need to have you thrown in jail to steal the story. I'll get it first anyway."

"Hang on a minute, I think I see a cop car down the road." He pulled off to the side and stopped.

"All right. Why are you calling, Hot Lips?"

"If we're still abiding by the bargain we made, I'm probably obligated to inform you of an interesting tidbit of information I came across at the university."

"Spit it out, babe. Get to the news."

"Second thought, I think I'll keep it to myself."

"Quit screwing around or I'll tell the police you stole the *Chronicle* credit card. You'll be stranded in California. Let's have it!"

"You really need to take a tranquilizer, McGraw. Or maybe a bottle of them. ... Harry Jerome has a son!"

"A son? There was no mention of that in the handouts Denton gave us. Are you sure?"

"An English professor remembers Jerome visiting the campus with his son — Harry Junior."

"Where is Harry Junior now?"

"I have no idea."

"All right. I'll check it out in Ukiah. What's your next move?"

"Trying to find someone else on campus who remembers Jerome or his son. Since it's Saturday, the university offices are closed. If they have Harry Junior's address I probably can't get it today."

"See you back at the hotel."

McGraw cruised past wine vineyards and pear orchards and finally reached Ukiah. The small, picturesque community seemed far removed from the turmoil of politics, yet it had produced a local boy, Harry Jerome, who might be destined to leave his mark on the world.

On the edge of town, McGraw noticed several people outside a diner. He pulled up nearby.

"Anyone know the way to Harry Jerome Junior's house?"

"No idea," one middle-aged man said.

McGraw wandered into the diner and asked to see a phone book. A "Harry Jerome" was listed on Fairview Court. McGraw called the number listed, but there was no answer.

He asked the group outside the diner how to get to Fairview Court.

"No idea," said the middle-aged man.

A shapely woman in her forties volunteered, "take Highway 253 north. It'll be on the left. It's not far from the airport."

"Much obliged," said McGraw.

"Why are you trying to find him?" asked the middle-aged man.

"No idea," said McGraw.

On Fairview Court, McGraw located the two-level ranch home and parked the Saturn in front. A Ford pickup sat in the driveway. McGraw hiked up to the porch and knocked on the door.

A blond, slightly overweight man wearing a tee shirt and jeans opened it. He seemed to be about thirty years old. "Can I help you?" he asked.

"Are you Harry Jerome Junior?"

"That's right."

McGraw did not realize it was Randall because he had never seen Moss' freelance troubleshooter.

"And your father is running for governor of Illinois?"

"That's right."

McGraw introduced himself. "You must be proud of your father."

Randall smiled. "I certainly am. He'll make a great governor."

Randall showed McGraw into the comfortably furnished living room and gestured toward a recliner. "Have a seat."

McGraw glanced around the room. An overstuffed armchair faced the television. The sofa was worn but still attractive. Several books rested on a small table nearby. It was a comfortable room, yet something bothered McGraw. He couldn't put his finger on it.

McGraw pulled a notepad and pen out of his sport coat.

"I'd like to ask you a few questions, Harry. How old are you?"

"Thirty-four."

"Lived in Ukiah all your life?"

"That's right."

"I'm surprised you aren't in Illinois, helping your father's campaign."

"I'd be there if he needed my help, but from what I hear he's doing well. I have commitments here, involving my wife Mary and my daughter Stephanie, but we're looking forward to visiting dad in the governor's mansion."

"I'd like to meet the rest of your family," McGraw said.

"Mary and Stephanie are visiting Mary's mother in San Diego."

"Well, maybe some other time … What kind of father was Harry Senior?"

"The best. Always there when I needed him. Kept a tight rein on me. Guess I turned out all right."

McGraw commented, "It must have been very hard on

you when your mother died in that automobile crash in Germany."

"Yes, it was. I was a student at San Jose State t the time. It was harder on dad, I'm sure. That's why he decided to leave Ukiah and take a job with the Farrell Foundation in Illinois. I stayed in California."

McGraw paused. "Why do you suppose your father's campaign literature doesn't mention that he has a son?"

"No mystery. He wants to protect my privacy—and my family's privacy."

McGraw posed several more questions, but it was obvious he wasn't going to get anything but "Ozzie & Harriet" answers about how great life with dad had been when Harry Junior was growing up in Ukiah.

As McGraw drove back down Highway 253 in the Saturn, he thought about his encounter with Harry Junior. Something wasn't right. Harry Junior was too much the average, loving son. And the living room still bothered McGraw … something was amiss. He pictured the room in his mind and tried to figure out what it was … and suddenly he knew. There were no photographs of Harry Junior and his family or Harry Senior. It was the kind of living room that normally would overflow with such family treasures, particularly since Junior's wife and daughter lived there, too.

On School Street, a battered wooden building caught McGraw's eye. A storm-ravaged sign identified it as the home of the *Ukiah Daily Standard*. Through the large front window McGraw could see someone working inside. He parked the Saturn and hiked up the front steps.

Inside the ramshackle building, a slender, middle-aged

man with unruly red hair pecked away at a keyboard connected to a computer. Absorbed in his work, he had not seen McGraw enter the newsroom.

"Excuse me, I wonder if—" McGraw said.

The bespectacled redhead jumped about six inches and spun around to face the intruder. He trembled noticeably. "What the hell do you want?"

"I didn't mean to startle you."

"'Course you didn't. That's why you snuck up on me."

"I'm David McGraw. I'm tracking down a story for the *Chicago Chronicle*."

"Albert Thatch, editor of the *Standard*."

They shook hands. Thatch offered McGraw a bottle of root beer, but McGraw declined.

"Do friends call you Red?" McGraw asked.

"Friends call me Albert. Only jerks think it's amusing to call every redhead they meet 'Red'."

"Don't hold back, Albert. Tell me what you really think."

Thatch laughed. "Subtlety never was one of my virtues. … *Chicago Chronicle*, eh? I bet you earn a helluva lot more than me and work a helluva lot less. I put in a sixty-five-hour week to get this rag out."

McGraw pulled up a chair and sat next to Thatch. "I work a forty-hour week when I'm not on special assignment, and yes, I probably make enough to buy and sell you three or four times. I belong to a union."

Thatch thought that over. "That's almost enough to make me stop writing editorials about greedy unions and join one myself. So what the hell you doing here?"

"Looking into Harry Jerome's background. He's running for governor of Illinois, you know."

Thatch glared at McGraw. "You're crazy. Harry runs an insurance agency down the street. Lives in Ukiah, and he's sure not running for governor of Illinois."

"Not Harry Junior. Harry *Senior*, his father. Harry Senior lived in Ukiah. He moved to Illinois fourteen years ago after his wife died in an automobile crash in Germany."

"Doesn't ring any bells. 'Course, I've only been in Ukiah about ten years. When I've talked to Harry Junior, he mentioned his wife and daughter. Never mentioned his mother or father. Seems like he would have told me if his father was running for governor of Illinois."

"I just talked to Harry Junior. He seemed proud of his father. ... Say, Albert, would you mind showing me what you have in your files about his parents?"

"So you want me to do your legwork for you. That figures. ... Wait here ..." Albert headed toward the back of the office mumbling, "Lazy, overpaid, big-city reporter."

"What did you say, Albert?"

"Nothin', McGraw. Make yourself comfortable."

Five minutes later, Thatch returned carrying two small folders that contained several clippings.

"This is what we've got, sport," Thatch said. "Here's the file on Harry's mother and father."

McGraw rifled through them. "An article from August 12, 1996 reports the Jeromes flew to Germany on a vacation, but nothing after that on either one of them. No obit on his mother. No more articles on his father."

"I noticed that," Thatch said, as he popped open a Coke can. "It seemed strange, so I looked up the bound newspaper files for August, 1996."

"And?"

"We haven't got them. They're missing."

"Missing?" McGraw repeated. "Does that happen often?"

"Never. I have no idea what happened to them." Thatch got up and reached for his suit coat. "The library should have the papers for that time period. They have our back issues on microfilm. C'mon, McGraw."

Thatch led the way as they strode briskly down the street until they reached the Ukiah Public Library. At the main desk, Thatch approached a gray-haired woman who seemed to be about seventy years ago.

"Gladys, this is McGraw. He's from Chicago, but he can't help it, so be nice to him. We need to see the *Standard* for August, 1996."

Gladys seemed puzzled. "Don't you have those files?"

"We should, but they seem to be missing."

Gladys led the way to a cabinet near the microfilm machines. She opened a drawer and rifled through the small boxes containing microfilm. Two months of the *Daily Standard* could easily fit on one roll.

"Just a moment," she mumbled. "That box must have been put in the wrong place."

She looked at the dates on all the microfilm boxes in the drawer, then opened another drawer and checked the dates on those boxes.

"I don't understand it," Gladys said, "but we don't have the *Standard* for August and September of 1996."

"That's quite a coincidence," McGraw noted.

"It's more than that," Thatch said. "It never happens."

While McGraw was in the library, he asked to see the most recent issue of the *Editor & Publisher Yearbook*, which listed facts about newspapers from across the country and around the world. In the section devoted to foreign newspapers, he looked up the listings for Berlin newspapers. He jotted down the names and telephone numbers of several of the papers.

As Thatch and McGraw departed from the library, Thatch suggested they go to see Harry Junior. "Harry might have saved some newspaper clippings describing the crash that killed his mother," Thatch noted.

The Ukiah editor led the way to Jerome Junior's house in his Chevy as McGraw followed in his rented Saturn. McGraw noticed rain clouds were moving in.

When McGraw and Thatch arrived at Harry Junior's abode, the pickup was gone. No one came to the door when McGraw knocked. No one could be seen through the windows.

"Tell me, McGraw ... What did Harry Junior look like?"

"Blond hair. About two hundred ten pounds. Said he was thirty-four years old."

"I don't know who you were talking to, but it wasn't Harry Junior. He has dark brown hair. Weighs about a hundred and eighty."

"What do you think is going on, Thatch?"

"You get the big bucks. You figure it out. I don't have any idea. ... You tell a strange story, McGraw. Tell you what—I'll keep my eyes open and see what I can find out. If I hear anything, I'll let you know."

McGraw wrote his cell phone number on a scrap of paper and gave it to Thatch. "I'll be going back to Illinois tomorrow."

As McGraw turned onto U.S. 101, which would take him back to San Francisco, he tried to make sense of what he had found in Ukiah. Who was impersonating Harry Junior?

Who were the people behind the charade, and what were they trying to hide? Was someone trying to keep McGraw from uncovering what happened in Germany in August of 1996? What had happened to the real Harry Junior and his wife and daughter?

McGraw had more questions and fewer answers than he did when he arrived in California.

Randall called Moss.

"McGraw was here. I was ready for him."

Randall filled Moss in on his conversation with the reporters.

"So you sent the Jerome Junior family on vacation but the editor, Thatch, could be a problem," Moss said.

"Right."

"Let me talk to Denton. I'll get back to you."

A few minutes later, Moss called Randall.

"Denton's squeamish about more killing," Moss said. "Keep the Jerome family on ice. I'll send someone out there to keep an eye on them and birddog the editor. When your relief gets there, fly home. Don't worry about McGraw. Wolfman will follow him when he hooks up with the girl."

"All this pussyfooting around. Why don't we whack 'em all and be done with it?" Randall suggested.

"Denton wants us to try it his way."

"What if it doesn't work?"

"Things will get messy."

13

McGraw returned to San Mateo shaken and tired. He found a note from Marilyn tucked under his door at the Bay Vista Hotel.

> McGraw,
>   I had time to kill after I got back from San Jose so I went shopping. Meet you at 7 tonight at the Harbor Village Restaurant in the Embarcadero Center. I'm in the mood for Chinese and the desk clerk said the Harbor Village's Cantonese dishes are out of this world.
>   Did you miss me?
>   Marilyn

McGraw banged his head against the door. Marilyn had gone shopping? Using what—the *Chronicle*'s credit card? Did she think they were in California for fun and games? They needed to find out what was going on fast. They didn't have time to stuff themselves with Chinese food.

McGraw took a deep breath and tried to relax. Well, they needed to eat somewhere. Might as well have Chinese food.

He showered and slapped Brut after shave on his face. Then, he slipped on tan khaki slacks and a black knit shirt. He didn't feel like trying to figure out where the Embarcadero Center was so he hailed a taxi to take him there.

McGraw arrived as Marilyn pulled up in her Camaro. She looked fresh as a daisy.

"Well, if it isn't the Queen of San Jose. Maybe you could tell me why you're shopping when we have work to do!"

Marilyn wheeled around to confront McGraw. "Don't give me a hard time, mister. I traipsed all over San Jose. I did everything I could! At least I found out he had a son. Did you do any better?"

"Not much," McGraw admitted, as he guided Marilyn toward the entrance. "Things were rather mysterious in Ukiah."

A waitress seated them at a table near an antique hand-painted vase that several people had used as an ashtray. The Harbor Village, owned by a Hong Kong restaurant, seated about four hundred.

Marilyn was in no mood for McGraw's musing about how things were "mysterious" in Ukiah. "Did you talk to Harry's son?"

"I did, and I didn't."

"Stop screwing around and tell me if you did, McGraw!"

"I spoke to a man who said he was Harry Jerome Junior. But the editor of the Ukiah *Standard* tells me the man I talked to was not Harry Junior."

"Who was he?"

"I have no idea. The editor is checking it out. Someone went to a lot of trouble to make me think I was talking to Harry Junior. And when I tried to find out more about the death of Harry's wife in that 1996 crash in Germany, I ran into a stone wall. The *Standard*'s files for that date are missing, and the Ukiah library's microfilm copies for those months are missing."

"That *is* strange."

Marilyn ordered sweet and sour pork, McGraw the broccoli and beef. He noticed Marilyn was looking lovely. He had never seen her in a dress before.

As they tackled the mai tais, Marilyn mentioned that she thought someone had followed her around the San Jose State campus. "I caught a glimpse of the guy. It might have been that goon in the army jacket."

"Murray Denton might have sent him. He knew I was flying to California."

"We've got to watch our step, McGraw! What's our next move?"

"We'd better get back to Illinois and start playing hardball. We've got to dig up a lot of answers, and we've only got nine days 'til the election."

As McGraw and Marilyn indulged in Chinese food, compliments of the *Chicago Chronicle*, Wolfman relaxed in his Jeep a block away. He called Moss on his cell phone. No answer.

It was time to make a decision, Wolfman concluded. Since he couldn't contact Moss, it was up to Wolfman. Well, sure, he could call Moss again, but that was a lot of trouble. Better to take care of the problem himself. The reporters had to be stopped. After all, wasn't that what he was being paid for? Enough of the screwing around. Time to take action.

He mused that Randall would handle things differently—Wolfman didn't mind leaving bodies lying around; Randall liked to get rid of them and tidy up—but Randall was still in Ukiah and this was Wolfman's show. He would waste the reporters and make it look like a robbery gone bad. Moss and Denton might squawk a little, but in the end they'd realize Wolfman had done the right thing. Probably give him a bonus.

A half hour later, Marilyn drove McGraw back to the Bay Vista in her rented Camaro. Marilyn retreated to her room to shower while McGraw called Slater.

"As I understand it," Slater said, after McGraw summarized the revelations of the last two days, "you still haven't found Harry Jerome. You discovered he has a son none of us knew about. You talked to the son, but you think he's an imposter. And, you can't find out anything about the crash that killed Mrs. Jerome because someone misplaced some microfilm. Is that it?"

"I suppose so."

"McGraw, you didn't get anything we can use! You wasted the trip out there! You blew the *Chronicle*'s money!"

"I knew you would be negative about this, Slater."

"It's hard to put it in a positive light. It doesn't make sense. Have you been drinking?"

"Do mai tais count?"

"Yes, McGraw, mai tais count. How many did you have? Forty-six? Forty-seven?"

"Only one. ... Listen, Slater, I'm giving you the straight story. You aren't right very often, but you were right about this: there are a lot of strange things about Jerome's campaign. If we don't find the truth, who will?"

Slater sighed. "I hate it when someone uses my own words against me. My first wife did that when she divorced me. ... All right. Check it out. Try to straighten out the confusion. And do it fast. You're spending a lot of time on this and wasting a bundle of the *Chronicle*'s money!"

If he thinks I'm wasting money now, McGraw thought, wait till he sees his next credit card statement.

"By the way, who paid for the mai tai, McGraw? You didn't charge it to the *Chronicle*?"

McGraw hastily hung up.

As McGraw flicked on the television set, Marilyn wrapped a towel around her in the adjoining room, feeling refreshed after a shower. She gazed through the door leading to the balcony and wondered if she would have time for a dip in the heated pool before they returned to Illinois. Hundreds of lights illuminated the city, while scores of headlights on the highway carved a path through the neon jungle. It all seemed to say, "this is where it's happening. There's more action here in a night than there is in Springfield in a year." Maybe it was time for Marilyn to move to a big city, where she could experience life in the fast lane.

Suddenly, Marilyn heard a creaking noise, like a door being opened slowly. She didn't pay much attention to it because she figured McGraw was opening a closet door in his room. Then, she heard the noise again. She realized it was coming from her room, from somewhere behind her. Her body tensed up. Her voice cracked as she asked, "Is that you, McGraw?"

She heard nothing.

The floor creaked again. She turned around ... and saw the sleazy man in an army jacket moving toward her with a pillow case stretched tight between his hands.

"McGraw!" Marilyn screamed.

Wolfman was nearly upon her when the door leading to McGraw's room swung open and McGraw burst in. He realized what was happening and grabbed a chair.

"Open the door!" McGraw shouted.

Marilyn managed to push open the door leading to the balcony. McGraw clobbered Wolfman with the chair. Wolfman staggered and sprawled out onto the balcony. He tried to grab the railing but missed. He stumbled and sailed over the railing. Marilyn and McGraw watched as he smashed into the top of a beach umbrella and plunged into the pool.

Two women in the pool and a half dozen people at tables around the pool screamed. When Wolfman surfaced he was bleeding but had survived the fall.

McGraw and Marilyn watched Wolfman struggling to reach the side of the pool as McGraw held her close. Her heart was beating wildly. Or was it his?

"It's all right now," he whispered.

They kissed, tentatively at first, then more passionately.

"Shouldn't we call the police?" she suggested.

"Absolutely."

He kissed her again.

"He might get away!"

McGraw didn't think the assailant was in any condition to run—or walk—but he called the police.

By the time three policemen and an ambulance arrived, Wolfman had staggered to his Jeep and fled. He left a trail of blood.

It happened so fast that the two reporters had not gotten a clear look at the assailant, but the army jacket found near the pool suggested it was the same man who had been tailing them. The reporters did not tell police about the mystery surrounding Harry Jerome and how that might tie in to the attempt on Marilyn's life. To the cops, it appeared to be a break-in that was thwarted.

When the officers left, McGraw lingered in Marilyn's room. It was an awkward moment.

"One of his buddies could come back," McGraw said. "It would be better if we got a different room and stayed together. Just so we're sure he doesn't come after you again."

Marilyn smiled. "I didn't know you cared, McGraw."

"Of course, I do. If we stayed here and he got you, I'd be in the next room. Easy pickings."

The desk clerk gave them a room on the fourth floor. They gathered their things and moved in.

Marilyn slipped into the same revealing pink negligee that had beguiled McGraw when they arrived in San Francisco. McGraw met her halfway and slipped his arms around her. He kissed her.

"I wanted to do that since the first moment I saw you," he said.

"You could have fooled me. You've been giving me a hard time."

"I know," McGraw conceded. "I've been under a strain lately. I met this crazy woman in Illinois ..."

He kissed Marilyn passionately and guided her toward the bed. That was the nice thing about hotel rooms. It wasn't very far to the bed.

"I normally don't do this on the first date," Marilyn purred.

"We haven't actually had a genuine, romantic date," McGraw reminded her. "You're doing it *before* the first date."

"Shut up, McGraw. You talk too much."

Later, in the still of the night, McGraw thought about the events that had brought him closer to Marilyn. She had moved in on his story; talked him into paying for her trip to California, the hotel room, the rented car and the dinner ... She was trouble. Now it was only a matter of time before his heart was ripped out. The only question was who would do it ... Marilyn, an assailant, or Slater.

The New McGraw wasn't doing much better than the Old McGraw.

14

The next morning, Marilyn and McGraw sprinted through a terminal at San Francisco International Airport and boarded a Chicago-bound United jet. Thirty minutes later, flight attendants doled out pastry and orange juice as the plane swept over northern California.

Marilyn leaned over and whispered, "We shouldn't do it again, McGraw."

McGraw looked up from the copy of *Illinois Business* he had been skimming. "Do what again?"

"What we did last night. We could screw up a perfectly good relationship. It's like we were saying at the restaurant the other evening. You and I should have a normal friendship without entanglements. I'm going to save myself for someone who respects me. Someone who can figure out the difference between romance and a workout at the gym."

"Don't blame me. You're the one that threw yourself at

me in that flimsy pink negligee. What was I supposed to do? Throw you out?"

Marilyn sighed. "Something like that. Only I didn't throw myself at you. You took advantage of me."

McGraw shook his head. "Look, in case no one ever told you, I'll tell you now: women don't take out billboards on Main Street saying 'for a good time, call Marilyn' unless they're ready to handle the action."

Aware other passengers were staring and smirking, Marilyn slipped lower in her seat. She whispered, "I was right all along, McGraw. You really are a terrible person."

A voice from the row of seats behind them said, "Who's Marilyn? Where's the billboard?"

Marilyn covered her face with her hands.

As the jet sped eastward over the midsection of Nebraska, McGraw and Marilyn considered what their next move should be in the quest to find the truth about Harry Ashley Jerome—fast. Without proof of wrongdoing, it wouldn't do much good to confront Murray Denton. He would say everything was fine. Jerome wouldn't tell them anything, either.

"We need to find out what's going on and who's behind it," McGraw noted. "Where is the real Harry Junior? Why the mystery about the crash in Germany? What happened to the microfilm of the *Standard*? And why are we being followed? What ties all this together? Is Jerome himself pulling a fast one—trying to fool Murray Denton and everybody else—or is there some sort of conspiracy? Let's rattle some cages and see what happens."

"What do you mean?" Marilyn asked warily.

McGraw reached into the pouch on the back of the seat in front of him and pulled out a copy of *Illinois Business* he had been looking at earlier. He turned to a full-page ad adorned with a photo of a smiling Harry Jerome. At the bottom appeared the line: "Paid for by the Committee to Elect Harry Jerome".

"We need to find out who's on the committee to elect Jerome. Then we'll squeeze the committee members. What do they know about Harry? Maybe they'll trip up and say something they shouldn't. Let's turn up the heat and see who sweats."

"That's risky," Marilyn suggested.

"I know. But we're running out of time. We've got to force the action."

"Shouldn't we find out what really happened in Germany in 1996?"

"Later," McGraw said.

At Chicago's O'Hare International Airport, McGraw and Marilyn boarded an American Eagle turboprop for the flight to Peoria.

The plane glided over fleecy clouds while Illinois farmland rolled by a few thousand feet below them. The flight to Peoria would last only about fifty minutes. By the time the plane finished taking off, it would be nearly time to begin landing. Marilyn noticed that most of the forty-two seats were occupied.

"In the old days, the planes didn't land in Peoria," the elderly man in the next seat told Marilyn. "The crew handed out parachutes to those wanting to get off in Peoria and the plane continued merrily on its way."

"I may look gullible, but even I don't believe that," she said.

"It's true," the old-timer assured her. "Once they were

late giving me a parachute and I landed in a wheat field in Kentucky."

Marilyn smiled, then turned to McGraw and whispered, "the guy next to me has completely lost it."

McGraw glanced at the old-timer. He seemed to be sleeping peacefully and appeared harmless.

"You're losing your grip on the ledge of life," McGraw suggested.

Marilyn, frustrated, poked the old-timer in the ribs with her elbow. "Tell my friend what you told me."

"What?" the old man murmured groggily. "What the hell do you want? Why can't you let an old man sleep?"

"This is not my day," Marilyn muttered.

IV

The German
Connection

15

McGraw and Marilyn fetched their baggage at the Peoria airport and retrieved the *Chronicle* Buick from the long-term parking area. Wally, the Channel 10 cameraman, had taken the station's van that Marilyn and Wally had used in Peoria back to Springfield.

McGraw and Marilyn journeyed south on Interstate 155 and hooked up with Interstate 55, which took them to Springfield, where Harry's campaign headquarters were located and where they would try to ferret out the secrets behind Harry's campaign.

As they neared the outskirts of Illinois' capital city that Sunday evening, McGraw and Marilyn passed another Jerome billboard, this one hailing him as the "Candidate for the Future." His face was plastered against a red, white and blue background.

"Maybe it should read 'the candidate without a past'," McGraw suggested.

Springfield, home to 116,000 people, was rich in Abraham Lincoln landmarks, including Abe's old house, the law offices and courthouse where he practiced law, and the tomb where he was buried. Lincoln had become a tourist industry, and distinguishing between the man and the myth could be as tricky as distinguishing between Moses and Charlton Heston. Had Lincoln really posed for postcards wearing an "I Love Illinois" tee shirt?

McGraw drove past a concrete building housing the Madden Collector Card Company. McGraw had seen Harry Jerome cards at a gas station, though he couldn't imagine why anyone would buy them.

"Look, it would be foolish for you to go back to your apartment in Springfield," McGraw said. "They might be waiting for you."

Marilyn looked at McGraw warily. "What did you have in mind?"

"We should find some place safe to hang out."

"We?"

"Well, sure. That way each of us would be sure the other was safe, and if we needed to move fast, we could."

"That's not a good idea. I told you we shouldn't get involved. I don't *want* to get involved with you."

"Don't worry. I've learned my lesson. We'll have adjoining rooms. It will be perfectly respectable. What do you say?"

"Only one room left," grumbled Maude Waddel, a gravelly voiced middle-aged woman with stringy brown hair. "Queen-size bed and a television. You want it?"

Maude was the owner and desk clerk at the Middle Westerner Motel on Stevenson Drive, on the south side of Springfield, and she was not being cooperative.

"Do you mind sleeping on the floor?" McGraw asked Marilyn.

"Do *you* mind sleeping on the floor?"

Another couple entered the motel office.

McGraw sighed. "We'll take it." He signed the register.

As McGraw and Marilyn headed for the exit, Maude examined the register. "Your room's around back, Mr. Slater."

After settling into room 122, Marilyn unpacked as McGraw flipped on an old Emerson television set. The horizontal hold wasn't holding. The picture rolled and rolled.

After succeeding only in speeding up the rolling, McGraw called the front desk.

"Have you tried adjusting the set?" Maude asked.

"Yep. Doesn't help."

"That's too bad. 'Course it's the risk you take, you know. We tell you there's a television in every room. We don't say whether it works. Look, do the best you can. Things are kind of busy. I've got a customer here who says he's Chief Justice of the Supreme Court, and he's demanding a room. I didn't know the Chief Justice was Japanese. If I give him my room, I might be bunking with you and the missus." And she hung up.

After dining at a Bonanza Sirloin Pit restaurant, McGraw and Marilyn returned to the motel room. Marilyn commandeered the bed.

McGraw lifted the blanket. "Scoot over."

"What do you think you're doing?"

"I can't sleep on the floor or in a chair," McGraw grumbled. "Bad back."

"Stay on your side, McGraw."

"No problem."

Minutes later they met in the middle of the mattress and made wild, restless love again.

16

At one in the morning, McGraw crawled out of bed, grabbed his cell phone and the list of telephone numbers he had copied out of the *Editor & Publisher Yearbook,* and locked himself in the bathroom. He dialed the country code for Germany (49), the city code for Berlin (30) and the telephone number of one of the newspapers, the *Kurier-Presse* of Berlin.

After several moments, he could hear the phone ringing.

"Guten morgen. *Kurier-Presse.*"

"Hello. I'm calling from the United States. Bitte, sprechen Sie Englisch?"

McGraw knew about four phrases in German and he had just used up one of them. He had not foreseen that the beginning German course he slept through in high school might actually come in handy one day.

"Nein. Einen moment, bitte," a woman said.

Moments later someone else came on the line.

"May I help you?" a woman said in a thick German accent.

"I would like to speak to a reporter or editor who speaks English."

"Hmmm. Wait, please."

In the bustling *Kurier-Presse* newsroom, the receptionist informed an editor that a caller from the United States wanted to speak to someone who spoke English.

"Whose English do you think is better?" Ernst Langer asked his assistant in German. "Hans's or Manfred's?"

"Manfred can read English, but he can't speak it worth a damn. Hans can probably muddle through."

"Hey, Hans!" Langer bellowed. "Take this call. Some guy in the States wants to talk to someone who can speak English."

"Don't give it to Hans," suggested Andrea, one of the reporters. "He can't even speak German without screwing it up."

"Muzzle her and throw her into the pound with the other dogs," Hans grumbled, as he returned to his desk and reached for the phone.

McGraw waited for someone to come on the line. Finally, he heard a male voice. The speaker sounded as though he were in his twenties or thirties.

"Good morning. This is Hans Montag."

"This is David McGraw, a reporter for the *Chicago Chronicle*."

"I have read your newspaper."

"What is your job at the *Kurier-Presse*?" McGraw asked.

"I am a reporter."

"That's great. I need help tracking down information for a story I'm working on."

"I will help, if I can."

"In August of 1996, there was a crash on the autobahn near West Berlin that killed Nancy Jerome. She was the wife of Harry Jerome of Ukiah, California. They were vacationing in Germany at the time. I need copies of the newspaper articles that reported the accident and her death."

"Nancy Jerome … Harry Jerome … August, 1996 … That should not be difficult. I will check our files for you."

"I need the information quickly." McGraw paused. "Please send it to me by e-mail. We will pay you for your time and expenses, of course."

"Give me your e-mail address," Hans said.

After McGraw hung up, he heard someone knocking at the bathroom door.

"McGraw! Who are you talking to in the bathroom at one in the morning?"

He unlocked the door and opened it. "I was calling my father. I didn't want to wake you."

"Really? How long has your father been in Germany?"

McGraw grimaced. "You eavesdropped again, didn't you?"

"I just happened to overhear you. But that's not the point. You were trying to find out what happened in Germany without me knowing about it! I thought we had an agreement! Fifty-fifty on the story!"

"That only applies to the American part of the story. Everything overseas is fair game."

"Don't give me technicalities, McGraw. We had an agreement!"

"All right. Don't get hysterical. I merely asked a reporter for the *Kurier-Presse* in Berlin to track down information about the crash that killed Mrs. Jerome."

Marilyn seemed satisfied. She headed back toward the bed. "Was that so difficult?" she said.

"You're pretty good at following people and prying secrets out of them. Did you ever work for the C.I.A.?"

"No, it comes naturally to the female sex."

McGraw's eyes opened wide. "Did someone say 'sex'?"

Marilyn got under the covers. "Forget it, McGraw. I'm tired. Go back to sleep."

17

When McGraw lived in Chicago, he occasionally visited newsstands that carried foreign newspapers. There, wedged between *The Observer* of London and *Le Monde* of Paris, he would find two quality papers from Germany, *Die Welt* and *Frankfurter Allgemeine*. Both dailies used very small headline type and a restrained, vertical page layout. They seemed to ooze respectability. They were the only German daily newspapers McGraw had seen, and he assumed Berlin's *Kurier-Presse* was similar to them.

He could not have been more wrong.

The *Kurier-Presse* was modeled after *Bild*, a German daily which had been founded by Axel Springer after World War II and which was a big moneymaker. *Bild* was cut from a completely different cloth than *Die Welt*, which also belonged to Springer's newspaper group. If *Die Welt* was Saks Fifth Avenue, *Bild* was the Little House of Horrors. Although it had sobered up a bit in recent years, *Bild* had long been known for flashy, jigsaw page layout; big, bold headlines; sensationalistic reporting; and photos of alluring, bare-breasted, scantily clad women. Over the years, it had sometimes played fast and loose with the facts if they got in the way of a good story. Occasionally, innocent people had been hurt. Novelist Heinrich Boll had written about *Bild*'s brand of sensationalistic journalism in his novel *Die verlorene Ehe der Katharine Blum* (*The Lost Honour of Katharina Blum*). And *Bild*'s reputation took another beating when an investigative journalist, Gunter Wallraff, secured a place on *Bild*'s staff for a few months and then exposed the paper's shortcomings in a book, *Der Aufmacher: Der Mann der bei Bild Hass Esser war*. But despite the problems with credibility, *Bild* continued to be startlingly successful. It was published in five cities and boasted a circulation of three and a half million.

Berlin's *Kurier-Presse* had been less successful, but by adopting *Bild*'s style of newspapering it had built up a circulation approaching 300,000 and a pile of money for its owners.

The *Kurier-Presse* was housed in a modern glass and concrete building near Friedrichstrasse, in the heart of Berlin. Like most other German newspapers, the *Kurier-Presse* was a morning journal. Hans Montag was one of a hundred reporters and editors who helped shape the paper each day. Hans, a graduate of the Institute of Publizistik—the journalism school—at the University of Munich, had come to the *Kurier-Presse* from Springer's *Bild am Sonntag*, where he had been a reporter for four years. Hans was well versed in the *Bild* style of newspapering that the *Kurier-Presse* had adopted.

When McGraw called at nine in the morning, Berlin time, the fifth-floor newsroom already percolated with activity, even though the paper would not go to press for another fourteen hours. Reporters and editors who worked on most of the inside pages put in fairly normal daytime working hours. Reporters and editors who handled breaking news often worked evening hours.

Hans tried to call a policeman in Munich in connection with a story about parking tickets, but he did not make contact—the policeman probably was on duty at Munich's Oktoberfest—so Hans put his story aside and wandered up to the *Kurier-Presse* library, where clippings from past issues were stashed. He told Rita, the woman on duty, that he wanted to see any clippings about Nancy Jerome, an American who had died in an autobahn accident in 1996.

A few minutes later, Rita handed Hans two clippings— page one of the *Kurier-Presse* for Friday, August 21, 1996, which contained an article and photo documenting the crash, and an article from *Die Welt*. Hans used the library's scanner to scan the newspaper page and the article into the computer. Then he sent McGraw an e-mail over the Internet, including the scans as attachments.

A few minutes later, Hans returned to the newsroom, where editor Ernst Langer lambasted him for being gone so long.

"Where have you been? I had a story for you, but I gave it to Andrea. I warned you about sneaking away when you are supposed to be working! If you don't do better, you'll be writing obits on a weekly in the hinterlands!"

"Promises, promises," muttered Hans.

18

Hans wrapped up his parking ticket story in Berlin at about the same moment Monday that a maid at the Middle Westerner Motel in Springfield, Illinois found Marilyn's panties under the bed and one of McGraw's socks in the bathroom sink.

"Animals!" she grumbled, in disgust.

At a diner down the street from the motel, McGraw and Marilyn wrestled with greasy fried eggs and washed them down with muddy coffee. A few minutes later, Marilyn used her cell phone to call Murray Denton at Eulenco. A "voice mailbox" recording informed her Denton would be barnstorming around southern and central Illinois with Harry the next three days. Marilyn and McGraw would confront Denton with their pressing questions when he returned.

In the meantime, McGraw drove Marilyn downtown to the State Board of Elections office, where campaign spending and disclosure reports were filed. Within a few minutes, they obtained a list of members of the Committee to Elect Harry Jerome—or COMTEJ, as it was known. The list included Foundation President Richard Dunnington; George Madden, CEO of the Madden Collector Card Company; Sue Ellen Jerrell; and Betsy French.

They knew who Dunnington and Madden were, and Sue Ellen Jerrell was that hotshot from suburban Chicago whose get-rich-quick videos probably would be aired on cable until the end of time, but who was Betsy French? Neither Marilyn nor McGraw had heard of her.

Back at the motel, the reporters discussed their next order of business—interrogating members of the committee. The idea was to light fires under them and then monitor the fallout to see who got burned.

Marilyn called Sue Ellen Jerrell in Winthrop Harbor, a Chicago suburb. Sue Ellen agreed to an interview Tuesday afternoon and gave Marilyn directions for finding the house. McGraw made an appointment to see George Madden Tuesday morning.

McGraw turned on his laptop computer and checked for e-mail. There was one message.

Marilyn peered over his shoulder. "From Germany?"

"Right."

The message contained a brief greeting from Hans:

> Enclosed are two attachments. Call me as soon as you get this.

That was followed by his cell phone number.

The files Hans had attached to his e-mail were graphics in TIFF format. McGraw launched Adobe Photoshop and opened the first file. It was a copy of page one of the *Kurier-Presse* dated August 21, 1981. Nestled between a photo of a very seductive young woman with knockers the size of cantaloupes and a story that seemed to be about an escaped tiger was:

NATO-FLUGZEUGE GESTARTET, NACHDEM EIN ALARM

Seitdem zwei amerikanische Touristen in einen todlichen unglück verwickelt.

Ein Chaos entstand in West-deutschland durch ein Autounfall, auf der Autobahn nahe Berlin, in dem zwei amerikanische Urlauber getoetet wurden. Die Opfer waren Harry Ashley Jerome und Ehefrau Nancy von Ukiah, California, USA. Beide waren von Drogen befallende Touristen die Lieferungen in Deutschland sabotieren wollten.

Das Jerome Auto knallte in eine Stark-stromleitung-Pole was eine fünf Stundenlang Stromunterbrech-ung verursachte. Die Polizei ist noch dabei den Vorfall nachzu-forschen.

McGraw scrutinized the page. A photograph under the headline showed a Volvo wrapped around a power pole. He could read neither the story nor the caption under the photo. He called Hans.

"I received the e-mail," McGraw said. "Thanks. So tell me what it says."

"It says there was a crash on the autobahn—"

"I knew that."

"—a crash that killed Nancy *and* Harry Jerome."

"What?"

"That's right."

"There must be some mistake. You must be talking about some other Harry Jerome."

"The article states very clearly that Harry Ashley Jerome and his wife, Nancy, of Ukiah, California, were killed in the crash."

"Good Lord," McGraw moaned.

"What did he say?" Marilyn demanded impatiently.

"You can't read German?" McGraw asked her.

"No. What did he say?"

"You're sure."

"Of course I'm sure. What did he say?"

"He said Nancy Jerome was drunk when she wrapped the car around the tree."

"You're lying, McGraw. The story says Harry and Nancy were *both* killed in the crash."

"I thought you couldn't read German!"

"Not very well. I had two years in college. I can read enough to get the gist of the story—enough to know you're trying to con me again!"

McGraw could hear laughter on the other end of the line.

"Your lady friend is smart, isn't she, Herr McGraw?" Hans asked.

"Not really," McGraw said.

"Maybe we should run a picture of her. Does she have nice boobs?"

McGraw examined them.

"They need to be inflated."

Marilyn grimaced. "All right, McGraw. Something tells me you're not talking about tires. ... You're talking about my breasts, aren't you, McGraw! You are rhino manure!"

"She is definitely bright," commented Hans. "I think I

love her. She is like a wild bronco waiting to be tamed. Could you arrange for me to meet her?"

McGraw was confused. The German newspapers he had seen were extremely conservative in design. They didn't run photos of topless women. And Hans, who seemed abnormally interested in earthy subjects, was a tabloid kind of guy. He was *National Exposer* material. Something was out of whack.

"Hans, I don't know how to phrase this delicately … what kind of newspaper is the *Kurier-Presse*?"

"Well, you know, Herr McGraw, there are different types of newspapers. Some are like *Die Welt*—conservative, restrained in layout, very careful with the facts. Others, like the *Kurier-Presse*, are closer to the masses. We have more of a common touch. We try to strike a responsive chord in our readers."

"Uh huh. You mean that you use huge headlines, racy stories and suggestive photos of scantily-clad women."

"That's right! You have papers like that, too!"

"Well, of course we have papers like that, but no self-respecting newspaperman would work for them."

Marilyn laughed heartily. McGraw ignored her.

"Really?" Hans said. "I thought the *New York Daily News*, the *New York Post* and some of your national supermarket weeklies were like that, and that they have large circulations."

McGraw wiped sweat from his brow. Had the motel room suddenly become very hot? "Well, yes, but the typical American newspaper is much more restrained and dignified, much more careful with the facts … I guess what I'm trying to say, Hans, is: can I believe the facts in your article, since your paper tends to exaggerate?"

"Relax, Herr McGraw. If you'll look at the other file

attached to the e-mail, you will find an article from *Die Welt* reporting the crash. It, too, says the crash killed Harry and Nancy Jerome. You can be assured it is absolutely true. Of course, there were some differences in how the papers reported the crash ..."

"Differences? What differences?"

"Well, let me look at the stories. ... Ja ... the *Kurier-Presse* said the crash knocked out the computers in Germany's defense facilities for five hours and NATO planes were scrambled in case it was the first stage of an enemy attack. It said Harry Jerome was a drug-crazed American bent on sabotaging West Germany's defenses."

"Holy crap."

"Now, here is the *Die Welt* article. ... Hmmm ... It says the Jeromes were tourists who had rented a car and went for a drive. The crash knocked down a street light."

"Look, are you sure Harry Jerome died in the crash?"

"Of course," Hans said haughtily. "I told you that. I would stake my reputation as a journalist on it!"

"Hans, you work for the *Kurier-Presse*. That isn't saying a helluva lot."

Marilyn laughed. "You tell him, McGraw! Tell him how you did things at the *National Exposer*."

McGraw ignored her. "Hans, is it safe to assume the *Die Welt* article gives an accurate account of what happened and the *Kurier-Presse* embellished on the facts?"

"Yes, certainly ... But why are you so interested in this? What is so important about Harry Jerome?"

"Nothing, except Harry Jerome is running for governor of Illinois."

"Oh! ... I see ... That is quite a trick," Hans suggested.

"Sure is," agreed McGraw. "How much do I owe you for all the help you gave us?"

"Nothing … if you give us the story. It could be quite interesting."

"It's a deal. But you can't print anything until we break the story."

McGraw hung up. He sat on the bed in their cramped motel room as Marilyn claimed the only chair.

"Hans has been nipping too much of the Lowenbrau," Marilyn said. "Harry Jerome can't be dead!"

McGraw shrugged. "I know it's shocking, but it would explain why we're being followed, and why someone didn't want us to see the *Ukiah Standard*'s story on the crash."

"Maybe, but I can't help thinking this is some colossal mistake."

"It's no mistake. it has been confirmed, and it's a helluva story. The stakes are high. If Harry Jerome is dead, the people behind Harry will do everything they can to make sure the word doesn't get out. That means you and I are expendable. Especially you."

"Why do you say that?"

"It wouldn't look good if they knocked off a Chicago reporter. If they got rid of a reporter for a piddling Springfield radio station, who would care?"

"Television station, McGraw! I work for a television station!"

"Oh, right."

Marilyn tried to be the Voice of Reason. It was a new role for her. "Before you go off the deep end, maybe there are other possibilities to consider. Perhaps Harry moved to Illinois, just like he says, but someone is trying to torpedo his candidacy by making it look like he died sixteen years ago and he's a fraud. Maybe that really was Harry's son in Ukiah, and the German newspaper articles are fakes. It would be easy to print up fake newspapers. Jerome might be the good guy in all this."

"No one could have known I would call the *Kurier-Presse*. Harry is dead, all right."

"So, who's running for governor of Illinois?"

"That's what we've got to find out," McGraw said. "When we confront Harry, we've got to get his fingerprints. In the meantime, we've got a lot of legwork to do. First, we'll contact Harry's backers and try to find out who's behind all this. Do the people on the committee realize they're supporting a dead man for governor?"

V

Run, Harry, Run

19

Marilyn and McGraw decided they had better tell their editors about the latest developments before they flushed out members of the committee to elect Harry.

McGraw called Slater from the motel room.

"Let me get this straight," Slater said. "Harry Jerome, the man who in all likelihood is going to be our next governor, does not exist. He and his wife died years ago in an automobile crash on an autobahn near Berlin, and someone is trying to get a dead man elected governor. Is that what you're telling me, McGraw?"

Why did it sound more reasonable when McGraw said it? "That sums it up, boss."

Slater's voice became noticeably higher. *"That's the craziest thing I've ever heard, McGraw!"*

"I've seen newspaper articles reporting his death! There's no doubt about it."

"Must be a case of mistaken identity," Slater suggested.

"I don't think so."

"I mean *you*, not Jerome. I sent a reporter named David McGraw out to find Harry Jerome. You are not David McGraw. You are some creature who landed in a cornfield in an alien spacecraft, and you are trying to mess up my mind. Or could it be that you're trying to save your ass by covering up the fact you can't find Jerome?"

"Slater, I'm telling you what I found. Now think about it. Isn't it a little strange that Jerome avoids the press, and that he's so hard to find? And remember—I've got photos of newspaper pages reporting Harry's death! A reporter at the *Kurier-Presse* in Berlin e-mailed them to me."

"Wait a minute. The *Kurier-Presse*?"

"That's right."

"Do you know anything about that paper, McGraw?"

"Yes. I heard the gory details."

"It's a rag. Sort of like a German edition of the *National Exposer*. Did you tell them you had worked for the *Exposer*? You could compare notes on UFO landings and Bigfoot sightings. I'm telling you, McGraw, you'd better make sure you've got your facts straight before you spread this around! Just because another paper printed the story doesn't mean we can accept it as gospel."

"Relax, Slater. My source sent me a copy of the story *Die Welt* ran on the crash, too, and that's a very highly regarded paper. There's no doubt."

Slater sighed. "You'd better be right, McGraw. If you're wrong, lawsuits and the loss of credibility will bury the *Chronicle*. ... And what am I supposed to tell Purnell? If I tell him Jerome is dead and someone else is running for governor, he'll throw me out on the street!"

"Well, don't say anything until I nail down the whole story."

"I still think there must be a logical explanation—two men with the same name, perhaps—but go ahead and check it out. Do it fast. And if it doesn't pan out, I'm going to see that all the expenses for this wild goose chase are taken out of your salary. You'll be working for nothing until hell freezes over!"

Marilyn insisted McGraw accompany her to Channel 10's offices in downtown Springfield to offer collaborative testimony when she talked to News Director Jed Runyon.

The newsroom was about twenty times smaller than the *Chronicle*'s. Television monitors mounted along the east wall carried programs from the major networks. Clocks stretched along the north wall gave the time for Tokyo, Moscow, London, New York, Springfield and Los Angeles. Five reporters hammered away at keyboards attached to desktop computers.

"Harriet!"

An excitable, thirtyish man with bushy brown hair shouted orders.

"Get over to city hall. The mayor's got an announcement about staff changes."

Harriet hesitated. "I don't suppose it could wait until my nails dry."

"*Get over there!*"

Harriet grabbed her coat and hurried out the door.

Marilyn approached the hyperactive editor. "I'm back. Jed!"

Runyon glared at her. "Well, look who decided to drop by—one of our political reporters. Long time no see, Marilyn. One more day and I was going to have your face plastered on milk cartons next to other Missing Persons."

McGraw was amazed. Runyon was like a little Slater, a baby monster in training to be a big monster.

"Try not to have a stroke, Jed. This is David McGraw, *Chicago Chronicle*."

They shook hands.

"There really is a McGraw? I thought Marilyn was feeding me a line so she could go to California."

"Of course there's a McGraw," Marilyn snapped. "Let's talk in your office."

Runyon led the way to a ten-foot-by-ten-foot room with glass walls.

"All right, so what happened?" he demanded. "Have you interviewed Jerome?"

"No, but we found out something that might interest you," Marilyn said. "Harry Jerome is dead!"

"What? He died? This morning? Why the hell aren't we covering the story?"

"He died sixteen years ago," Marilyn said. "In the same automobile crash in West Germany that killed his wife."

Runyon breathed deeply. "Look, if you wasted your time out there, admit it, but don't fabricate ridiculous stories!"

McGraw retrieved copies of the *Kurier-Presse* and *Die Welt* articles from his briefcase and showed them to the chief.

"What is this supposed to prove?" Runyon bellowed. "I can't read German! They could say 'April Fool, news director—you're a jackass' and I wouldn't know the difference."

Marilyn shrugged. "That's what happened last April Fool's Day when the newsroom gang had a fake newspaper printed in Spanish." She pleaded with Runyon: "We're telling you the truth. These stories were published in German newspapers sixteen years ago. They prove Harry and Nancy Jerome both died in an autobahn accident!"

"It's just not possible," Runyon said. "Are you two on drugs?"

"No, Jed," Marilyn assured him.

"Uppers? Downers? Horizontals?"

"No, Jed."

"Well, you must be on something. You can't be serious. Harry Jerome—the foundation president, the candidate, the hero—is a fake? An imposter?"

"That's the way it looks. McGraw and I are still chasing the story. And when we nail it down, it will be a dynamite exclusive! It will put our little podunk station on the map!"

"What?"

"Sorry. I've been hanging around McGraw too much."

"If Harry Jerome is dead, who the hell is running for governor? Who's running around the state using his name?"

"That's what we've got to find out," McGraw said.

"Well, I'll put Eric on day-to-day coverage of the Jerome campaign. You can follow this up, Marilyn. Just stay in touch. And you'd better be one thousand percent sure of your information before it's aired."

"We won't go with the story until we're sure."

"Can you wrap it up before the election?"

Marilyn shrugged. "If we don't, Illinois may elect a dead man as its governor!"

"Nervous, isn't he," McGraw muttered, as he followed Marilyn through the newsroom. "Reminds me of someone I know back at the *Chronicle*."

Marilyn paused at her desk to check her mail. McGraw

pulled a copy of the photo of Jerome shaking hands with John Wayne out of his briefcase.

"I wonder how they did this," he said.

Marilyn studied it. "It sure doesn't look like a fake."

She took the photo over to Steve Alton, a video editor who was talking to the assignment editor.

"Steve, take a look at this photo."

Alton examined it closely.

"What about it?"

"Could it be a fake?" Marilyn asked.

He studied it more intently. "A few years ago I would have said no. But things have changed. Come along."

As they headed toward an editing room, Marilyn introduced McGraw to Alton. Once in the room, Alton took the photo from Marilyn and scanned a digital copy of it into the computer using a photo scanner. Then he scanned a photo of the President into the computer. Finally, he opened a video retouching software program and began working with the photos, cutting Harry Jerome out of the John Wayne photo and placing him in the photo with the President. He kept working on the background—duplicating part of the background, erasing unneeded parts—until he had created a new picture. This one showed Harry Jerome and the President together.

"Because of software like this, it's difficult to spot a forgery. It's easy to take any legitimate photo and make it into a lie. Then you can print the thing out at high resolution on glossy photo paper and you won't be able to tell it from a real photo. So, to answer your question—it very easily could be a fake."

Alton gave Marilyn and McGraw printouts of the photo showing Jerome standing next to the President. When the time came to break the story, the photo of Jerome and the

President would illustrate the point that it was possible to fake photos.

"But remember," Alton cautioned the reporters as they left the newsroom, "just because the photo could have been faked doesn't mean it was. You need proof!"

20

McGraw dropped Marilyn off at her apartment and she retrieved her red Mustang from the parking lot. A few minutes later she began the journey to Winthrop Harbor to confront Sue Ellen Jerrell. McGraw headed for southwest Springfield to interview George Madden, another Jerome supporter.

The air was cool, tinged with a touch of winter, as McGraw breezed along in the Buick. The roads cut a path through acres of towering oak and birch trees adorned with dazzling red and gold leaves. Squirrels scampered across the ground. As McGraw passed a junior high school, he could see youngsters playing football.

The Madden Collector Card Company was housed in the single-story concrete structure on the edge of Springfield that McGraw and Marilyn had passed on their way into the city. The sign in front resembled a huge baseball card, featuring a balding, smiling, fiftyish bear of a man swinging a baseball bat.

The lobby was lined with blowups of cards the Madden Company had issued over the past fourteen years—sports cards, including rare Wayne Gretzky and Michael Jordan sets, as well as such nonsport cards as Major Battles of the Korean War and the Harry Jerome Collection.

McGraw was escorted to a reception area outside George Madden's office, where he flipped through a brochure describing the company and its cards as he waited for Madden to see him.

When a secretary ushered McGraw into Madden's office, McGraw realized Madden was indeed the balding, fiftyish man whose photo was plastered on the sign out front.

"Have a pack of Harry Jerome cards," Madden said. "They're selling like crazy in Chicago."

McGraw relaxed in a black, foam-covered chair and opened the pack. The cards depicted the usual highlights of Harry's career, including the convenience store holdup and the familiar photo of Harry shaking hands with John Wayne.

"Card collecting has changed since you were a kid, McGraw. The business is more competitive now. There's gold stamping, ultra-violet coating and embossing. And runs are often limited to excite collectors. By limiting the runs, the cards become valuable sooner. In fact, a rare 24-karat gold card inserted randomly in a pack could be worth quite a bit before a year is out."

McGraw hadn't realized cards had become such big business. "Why do you distribute Harry Jerome cards? Why not Governor Dodge cards? He's more widely known."

Madden smiled. "Because I own the company and I wanted to do it. I like Harry Jerome. I support him. And I thought, what the hell. If Harry Jerome cards can help

Jerome become more widely known and win him a few votes, why not do it."

A soft knock on the door interrupted them. The secretary peeked her head inside. "May I see you a moment, Mr. Madden?"

Madden got up from his desk. "Excuse me, McGraw. Business. Probably about the Dallas quarterback I just signed to an exclusive contract. If he autographs anything without my approval, I can have his legs broken."

McGraw wasn't sure if Madden was joking. He made a mental note to read the fine print before signing a contract with Madden.

While Madden conversed with his secretary in the outer office, McGraw glanced at Madden's desk. It was littered with reports and correspondence. He noticed a press release printed on paper bearing the letterhead of The Christian Majority for Jerome:

November 4

SHOCKING NEW REVELATIONS ABOUT GOV. DODGE SHOW WHY HARRY JEROME MUST WIN THE ELECTION!

Disclosures about Illinois Governor Stephen Dodge's marital infidelity make it even more urgent for Christians to join together to elect Harry Jerome to the governorship in Illinois.

News reports circulating this weekend revealed Governor Dodge had engaged in an adulterous liaison with Kathleen Nordstrom, an aide on the governor's staff, over a period of four years.

"I am shocked by this news," Jerome said. "It is a sad day for the entire state.

This episode illustrates clearly why new moral leadership is needed in Illinois."

The Rev. Lawrence Drury, president of the Christian Majority for Jerome, said the disclosures show the country is at a crossroads. "Christians cannot sit idly by while corrupt, liberal politicians lead the nation down the primrose path to ruin," Drury proclaimed.

You can do your part now by supporting the election of Harry Jerome. Send what you can—$500, $100, $50, even $1, if that's all you can afford—to help us get the word out. Or, if you wish, call 1-800-H JEROME to make your donation. Have your major credit card ready ...

McGraw was stunned. There had been no allegations about Dodge having an affair. Then he noticed the date in the upper right corner—November 4. The mailing would not go out for four days. Pastor Drury and George Madden knew in advance the allegations were going to be leveled against Dodge! Either they had psychic powers or something underhanded was going on.

McGraw was about to grab the press release and slip it into his shirt pocket when Madden breezed back into his office. "Sorry for the delay, McGraw. Now, how can I help you?"

McGraw settled back in his chair.

"I'm doing a story on Jerome. 'The Man Behind the Myth' kind of thing. How long have you known him?"

Madden plopped his feet atop his large oak desk. McGraw was tempted to do the same until he recalled Madden's remark about breaking the quarterback's legs.

"Harry and I have been good friends for years," Madden said. "We've served on many committees together."

McGraw noted that in his notebook. If Jerome indeed turned out to be a fraud, quotes like that would have Madden twisting in the wind with him. It would serve Madden right for telling such outrageous lies to a reporter.

Madden continued: "He's a director of this corporation, you know. Harry's a modest, unassuming, extremely capable man who decided to run for office when he realized Governor Dodge's anti-business policies and tax hikes were draining the state's revenues. The governor's decision to block the billion-dollar Hudson Entertainment and Communications Center was the last straw. That project would have provided employment for thousands! Harry felt it was his civic duty to give up his privacy and personal comforts to serve the public in this time of crisis."

"He didn't give up very much privacy," McGraw noted.

"But Harry is more than a public servant. He's a warm, caring human being. He'll beat the socks off you on the golf course, then spend the night with you at the hospital when your wife is undergoing gall bladder surgery. Yes, when they made Harry, they broke the mold."

Don't be so sure, McGraw thought. There seem to be two of him.

"Harry is the perfect candidate for the new millennium, McGraw," Madden continued. "The state's damn lucky he decided to run for governor, and next week he's going to win the election. You can quote me on that."

McGraw did. "I notice you're on the Committee to Elect Jerome," he said.

"That's right."

"Are you one of the big contributors to the Jerome campaign?"

"I have helped support it, yes."

"I notice Betsy French is on the committee. I haven't heard of her. Who is she?"

"An ordinary citizen. It's important to have them represented, too."

"Where does she live?"

"Carbondale, maybe. Or Champagne. I'm not sure."

"Did Harry play football at San Jose State?" McGraw asked.

"Yes, I believe he did. You've done your homework, McGraw!"

"I try, George. And after college, Harry returned to Ukiah, California?"

Madden nodded contentedly. "That's right."

Now that the big rat was nibbling the cheese, it was time to spring the trap.

"You seem to know a lot about the candidate. Are you aware that a man named Harry Ashley Jerome of Ukiah, California, died in a crash on a West German autobahn sixteen years ago?"

"It was *his wife* that died, McGraw."

"No. Newspapers in Germany reported that Harry *and* his wife died in the crash."

Madden's face tightened and became flushed. He was angry. "You'd better get your facts straight, McGraw. It would be a big mistake to spread rumors and lies about Harry Jerome. Those who play with fire get burned. Do you understand, McGraw? There is no room in this campaign for sleazy, irresponsible tabloid journalism."

Did Madden know McGraw had worked for the *National Exposer* or was that a stab in the dark?

Madden buzzed for a security man. "This interview is over, McGraw! I'll be talking to your publisher about you!"

"Would you? I can never get in to see him."

"Get outta here!"

As a security man escorted McGraw to an exit, the reporter could hear Madden on the phone:

"That's what he said ... died on a German autobahn!"

As McGraw was rushed out a side entrance, he advised the security man to leave, too. "God's going to bring this building crumbling to the ground any second," McGraw insisted. "I haven't heard lies like this since my father told my mother he hadn't been drinking—his clothes smelled of liquor because he was walking past a distillery when it exploded."

21

That afternoon, Marilyn guided her Mustang along a private road leading to a rambling, Tudor-style home in Winthrop Harbor, a town abutting Lake Michigan north of Chicago. Marilyn had no idea the house and estate would be so lavish. Sue Ellen must have stumbled onto the secret of wealth, for she was living The Good Life. Why would she jeopardize it by joining Harry Jerome in criminal activities?

Marilyn rang the doorbell. Moments later, Sue Ellen opened the door wearing a bathrobe.

"Marilyn?"

"That's right."

"Come in! I'm Sue Ellen Jerrell."

Marilyn was struck not only by the spacious, ornately decorated rooms but also by the television cameras and equipment set up in the living room.

"You have a beautiful home," Marilyn said.

Sue Ellen laughed. "This isn't my home, honey. I'm renting it for three days for the taping of my next half-hour info-mercial. I live in a three-bedroom house in Glen Oak."

"Isn't that misleading?" Marilyn said. "The people who watch your show have the impression this is your home."

"And so it is. For three days. Honey, I make a lot of dough, but I can't afford a house like this. If I did my sales pitch from *my* home, no one would fork over two hundred and forty-nine dollars for my video cassettes. ... Have a seat. I'll be back in a few minutes. I've got to get ready. The film crew will be here in a half hour."

As Sue Ellen put the finishing touches on her makeup, Marilyn nosed around the kitchen and the sunken living room in the sprawling home.

Several minutes later, Sue Ellen returned wearing a white suit with gold trim and gold accents.

"Your clothes are gorgeous," Marilyn noted.

"Thank you. Fortunately, I can write them off as a business expense. They're props for my videos, just like the house. ... Now, what can I help you with? You said something about Harry Jerome."

They sat in the living room on a plush white sectional sofa that stretched from one end of the room to the other.

"I was surprised to see you listed as a member of the committee to elect Jerome."

Sue Ellen shrugged. "Murray Denton told me they needed a prominent name from upstate Illinois on the committee, and since I'm sympatico with Harry's political views, I was happy to cooperate. Besides, I was assured I wouldn't have any duties."

"Have you met with the other committee members?"

"No. Being on the committee was just a formality, they said."

"Who is Betsy French?"

"Betsy French … Don't believe I've ever heard of her."

"She's on the committee to elect Harry, along with Reverend Drury, Richard Dunnington, George Madden and you."

"Well, as I said, the committee has never gotten together."

"How well do you know Harry Jerome?" Marilyn asked.

Sue Ellen seemed to choose her words carefully. "We are good friends. As you probably know, Harry is on my board of directors. He's an extraordinarily gifted executive who has worked behind the scenes for civic improvement for years. He'll make an outstanding governor."

Sue Ellen paused, pleased Marilyn was writing down her statement word for word.

"Do you run into Harry often?" Marilyn asked. "Do you see him at business meetings, or socialize with him?"

"We run into each other quite often when we're in the same part of the state. Harry asked me to appear at the big Election Eve rally he's planning in Chicago, and I'm thrilled about it."

"Have you noticed anything unusual about Harry? Does he sometimes seem *too* perfect?"

"I'm not sure what you mean."

"Harry must have faults. I never met a man who didn't."

Sue Ellen smiled. "Neither have I. But I'd say Harry is about as close to being perfect as the male of the species can be."

Marilyn smiled slyly. "Do you know much about his background?"

"I know he grew up in California and moved to Illinois

after his wife's death to manage the Farrell Foundation. I hear he did a terrific job there."

The ringing of a telephone interrupted them. Sue Ellen excused herself and took the call in the dining area. Marilyn could see Sue Ellen's reflection in a mirror and overheard what she was saying …

"I can't talk now. There's a reporter here. … Marilyn Westley. I believe she's with a Springfield television station … Calm down, Murray. I haven't said anything but what a great guy Harry is. Why are you bent out of shape? … Well, how was I supposed to know she's out to get Harry? I thought she was just doing a feature story on him. What's this all about? … *Problems?* What problems? You told me there wouldn't be any! My reputation is at stake, hotshot. We need to talk! … All right. I'll call you later."

Marilyn decided the "Murray" that called Sue Ellen had to be Murray Denton.

As Sue Ellen returned to the living room, the doorbell rang. When she opened the front door, three men carrying video equipment entered.

"Go ahead and set up," she told them.

Sue Ellen returned to the sofa where Marilyn was sitting. "Sorry for the interruption, honey. Look, the camera crew is here and I've got to go over the script. Sorry to rush you, but I really don't know anything else to tell you about Harry Jerome."

"I see," Marilyn said. "Well, I'll tell you something strange. A few days ago a colleague of mine discovered that Harry Jerome died in an automobile crash sixteen years ago in West Germany! Maybe you could explain why you are on a committee that's trying to put a dead man in the governor's office."

Sue Ellen's composure was shaken. "That's the most absurd thing I've ever heard. Obviously you've got Harry Jerome confused with someone else. Now, if you'll excuse me, I've got things to do."

Marilyn dawdled at the far end of the living room as the crew prepared to tape the infomercial. Within a few minutes, cameras rolled and Sue Ellen turned on the charm …

"The key to unlocking the treasures of this world lies in the Five Great Secrets of Success. With these secrets, you can turn your life around! No more wishy-washy, namby-pamby excuse-making and procrastinating—you'll be in charge of your own destiny! And, friends, you won't find these Secrets of Success anywhere else. You can only find them here, and they're free when you order my videos for only two hundred and forty-nine dollars. Isn't that a cheap price to pay for success! Why, you'd pay more than that for a good living room chair."

Sue Ellen could be convincing. When she threw in six steak knives as another free bonus, Marilyn was hooked. But Marilyn didn't have the two hundred and forty nine dollars with her, so she returned to her Mustang.

On the drive back to Springfield, Marilyn switched on the car radio. A Chicago station was airing a promo for a television program …

"Tonight, on Hudson Cable Television's Movie & Entertainment Channel—an hour-long special chronicling the exciting life of Harry Jerome, including his boyhood in California, his days as a college football star, his heroics in the military and his courageous confrontation with the holdup man who tried to kill him. It's the heroic life story of the man who will, in all likelihood, be the next governor of Illinois. Don't miss it!"

Marilyn was sure of one thing: the journalists working for Martin Hudson weren't doing their jobs. They were Harry's biggest cheerleaders.

22

Marilyn returned to the Middle Westerner Motel in Springfield Tuesday evening and compared notes with McGraw about their encounters with Sue Ellen Jerrell and George Madden.

"Sue Ellen knows Harry isn't what he's supposed to be, but I don't think she knows everything that's going on," Marilyn said. "She got rattled when I suggested that Harry faces an uphill battle, since he's been dead for more than a decade."

"Very subtle."

"And Murray Denton called her while I was there. I think he chewed her out for agreeing to see me."

"Madden knows more than he's telling, too."

McGraw described the flyer on Madden's desk from The Christian Majority for Jerome condemning Dodge for marital infidelity.

"What business is it of Drury's if Dodge had an affair?"

"That's not the point. There haven't been any reports

of an affair between Dodge and his secretary. The charges haven't been aired yet—but Madden and Drury already have figured out how they're going to react to them."

"Ohhh. You caught them with wet ink on their fingers, so to speak."

"We need to find out if Reverend Drury is one of the brains behind Harry's campaign or somebody's pawn, and time is running out. Let's pay Drury a visit tomorrow morning."

"You're taking me to church, McGraw? How sweet. Are you going to make an honest woman of me by marrying me?"

McGraw laughed. "It would take more than that to make an honest woman out of you."

McGraw was in the doghouse again.

As Marilyn slept, he switched on the television. On the rolling screen, Bruce Balboa urged listeners to come down to Balboa's Deluxe Used Cars before midnight for "the lowest price ever on a DeSoto." That was followed by a new Jerome for Governor commercial.

"Governor Dodge raised business taxes," the voiceover was saying. *"Harry Jerome will lower taxes and encourage investment. Governor Dodge wants to keep welfare benefits intact. Harry Jerome will reduce them. The choice is yours—re-elect a governor who drove business out of Illinois, or elect Harry Jerome and propel Illinois into a new era of prosperity! Paid for by The Committee to Elect Harry Jerome."*

"Yes, but Governor Dodge is alive," McGraw said. "Harry Jerome is dead. The choice is yours. Paid for by the *Chicago Chronicle* and Channel 10."

A voice was heard coming from the bed. "Cute, McGraw. Now turn off the television and come to bed!"

23

WEDNESDAY, NOVEMBER 1
6 days before the election

The sandy-brick First Church of Eternal Life occupied a block on Springfield's Grand Street.

In the foyer, Marilyn browsed through a flyer describing the church. "More than two thousand people attend services here," she told McGraw. "Drury's sermons are aired on radio and television stations across the country."

They heard a booming, disembodied, apocalyptic voice. It seemed to come from the main worship hall.

As they entered the worship area, they marveled at the rows and rows of pews which could hold more than a thousand people for each worship service. Television equipment was stationed strategically throughout the cavernous hall. It contrasted sharply with Springfield's small First Presbyterian Church, where Abraham Lincoln's family worshipped in the 1850s.

A slender man at a podium in the front of the worship hall seemed to be the source of the thunderous voice.

"It's no use trying to hide," the voice boomed, cascading from wall to wall. *"Satan will find you. Your only hope is to turn to God."*

"Was that a preacher or did I just have a religious experience?" McGraw asked.

"That was a preacher."

At the podium, the slender man looked up. McGraw thought the man might be looking to the heavens, but he had his eyes on a small television control room tucked away in the distance, fifteen feet above the pews.

"How is the voice level?" the preacher asked.

A voice came back over a loudspeaker: *"Very good."*

The pulpit was so far from the back of the church where McGraw and Marilyn were standing that they could not make out the features on the face of the man standing at the microphone. The reporters started down the center aisle. When they drew near the pulpit, Marilyn called out, "Excuse me … We are looking for Pastor Drury."

The slender man descended a flight of steps to the worship floor. "I am Pastor Drury. How can I help you?"

Drury had gray hair and wore pince-nez glasses. He seemed to be about sixty.

Marilyn and McGraw introduced themselves.

"We notice you've launched an organization to help elect Harry Jerome," Marilyn noted.

Drury nodded. "That's right."

"I'm surprised a clergyman would become so involved in a political campaign," she said.

"Well, I think it's very important that Harry Jerome be our next governor. It's the only way we can keep this state on the path to moral integrity and prosperity! I wanted to do my part to help him."

"Have you met Harry Jerome?"

"Of course. I've known Harry about ten years."

"Ten years?" McGraw and Marilyn repeated in unison.

"Well, maybe nine years."

"You've seen him often over the last few years?" Marilyn asked.

"Of course. He attends this church whenever he's in town."

"You're really putting your church behind Jerome," Marilyn noted. "Television appeals and mass mailings ..."

"The Christian Majority for Jerome feels it is important that a God-fearing Christian be in the governor's house."

"We've got one there," McGraw pointed out. "Governor Dodge is a Christian. Or doesn't that count?"

"Just calling oneself a Christian is not enough, Mr. McGraw."

"I see. A person must pass your litmus test to be not only a Christian but a *true* Christian."

"I don't like your insinuation, McGraw. I believe the Bible is the Word of God. It is the source of all truth. I look to the Bible for divine guidance."

Marilyn grimaced. "Do you really think Jesus would want you to support candidates who make life easier for the rich and harder for the poor? Jesus encouraged love and compassion, not selfishness and greed."

"Look, I don't have time to discuss politics with you," Drury said, "and I don't believe you are qualified to discuss theology. After you have spent several years in a seminary and several years preaching The Word, come back and we'll talk."

Drury turned and started back to the pulpit.

"I suppose you're going to be hitting the issue of Governor Dodge's alleged infidelity pretty hard," McGraw said.

Drury stopped abruptly and turned around.

"I don't know what you're talking about, McGraw. There have been rumors, of course."

"It seems strange that your organization has a mailing ready to condemn Dodge for marital infidelity—only he hasn't been accused of it yet."

"You're mistaken, McGraw. Do you have a copy of this alleged mailing?"

"No, but—"

"Then I suggest you not spread such rumors."

"We have been doing some investigating," McGraw said. "Let me tell you what we know for sure—Harry Ashley Jerome of Ukiah, California *is dead*. ..."

Drury flinched. McGraw rambled on.

"Some people are spending a trainload full of money to elect as governor a man who has assumed Jerome's identity. You seem to know about allegations that Governor Dodge had an affair even though no such allegations have been made. And you say this dead man has been attending your church for nine or ten years. You talk a lot about morality, but you are in this up to your eyeballs."

"That's outrageous, McGraw," Drury stormed. "That's the most ridiculous thing I've ever heard. You're doing everything you can to smear a great man—a man who will be elected governor of Illinois in a few days. I advise you not to make any more unsupported allegations. *It could be very dangerous for you!*"

24

Harry Jerome and his top advisors had moved on to Murphysboro, a small town in southern Illinois where a few hundred people turned out for a picnic. The lure was free food, but a few people might decide to vote for Jerome. It was Jerome's last swing through southern Illinois before the final push began in the Chicago area, Springfield and Peoria.

Denton was sampling hot dogs, potato salad and watermelon when his cell phone rang. It was Roger Moss.

"Those snooping reporters confronted Drury, Madden and Sue Ellen Jerrell. We've got to eliminate them before they blow the lid off the campaign!"

"Who? The reporters?"

"Yes. The reporters!"

"Cool off, Moss. They don't have anything they can use."

"We can't let 'em run around stirring things up. If they find something to confirm their suspicions, it may be too late to stop them."

"I'll drive back to Springfield today. Don't do anything 'til we talk!"

Denton warned Jerome and Jamieson not to answer reporters' questions. Then Denton checked out of his motel in Murphysboro and headed back to Springfield in his Lexus.

The drive gave Denton time to ponder how a carefully orchestrated political campaign suddenly found itself facing disaster. The main culprit, of course, was Morton Searcy. He had used a real man as the basis for Harry's resumé and then apparently was driven by a guilty conscience to defect. But it was a little late to worry about Searcy. Events had spiraled out of control, and the problem now was how to contain the damage and win the governorship on election day. David McGraw and Marilyn Westley had to be stopped— Moss was right about that—but Denton did not want more bloodshed. Was there an alternative?

Marilyn called Eulenco at two that afternoon asking when Denton would return to Springfield. The secretary said Denton had just walked in the door. Denton picked up a phone and invited the two reporters to drop by.

A half hour later, Denton greeted McGraw and Marilyn in the lobby of the Eulenco building. He led them into his office and closed the door. McGraw noticed the far wall was adorned with a "Bedtime for Bonzo" movie poster, with Ronald Reagan's name prominently displayed; a large photo showing the first President Bush throwing up on the prime minister of Japan; and a tabloid front page reporting one of President Clinton's affairs with a young woman.

Denton didn't waste time on pleasantries. "I don't like what I've been hearing—that you're spreading outrageous stories about Harry Jerome being dead," Denton told the reporters. "Some of Harry's supporters are understandably upset. They asked me to have a talk with you before this gets out of hand."

"Good," McGraw said. "Maybe you can set us straight. How does it happen that Harry Ashley Jerome—who grew up in Ukiah, played football at San Jose State and died on an autobahn in Germany sixteen years ago—is now running for governor of Illinois? This is a helluva story! Proof there's life after death! We've got a dead man running for governor!"

"That's absurd," Denton scoffed. "You're way off base. It's some sort of mistake or misunderstanding. There must be two Harry Ashley Jeromes."

"This isn't a game," Marilyn insisted. "We've got a lot of questions to ask Harry and we aren't going to play hide and seek with him 'til after the election. When do we talk to him?"

"Harry is campaigning in southern Illinois. I'll give the two of you an exclusive interview with him as soon as possible. He'll clear up any confusion about these ridiculous allegations. In the meantime, don't spread any more outrageous lies! Where did you come up with the absurd idea Harry Jerome is dead?"

"I've got proof," McGraw asserted, with the confidence of a poker player holding a royal flush. "These are articles from German newspapers reporting the death of Harry Jerome of Ukiah, California in 1996."

Denton shook his head. He did not seem as confident as

he had before. "Obviously the Dodge people are up to their dirty tricks and you've swallowed it hook, line and sinker. Harry will set you straight."

"Who is Betsy French?" Marilyn asked.

Denton was caught off balance, like a batter thrown a curve ball when he expected a fastball, but he recovered quickly.

"A housewife who agreed to serve on the Committee to Elect. She symbolizes Jerome's grassroots support."

"Where does she live?" McGraw said.

"I'm not sure. Joliet, maybe." Denton decided to take the offensive and turn on the charm. "As long as you're here, would you like to see our operation? You'll find there's nothing evil or mysterious about it. We've got nothing to hide."

McGraw and Marilyn had been hoping Denton would give them a tour of Eulenco. Somewhere in the bowels of the building might lie the truth about Harry Jerome and his campaign.

Denton led the reporters down a long, wood-paneled hallway. He paused outside the Computer Division, which housed a half dozen powerful mainframes.

"These babies give us the power of supercomputers," Denton said. "State-of-the-art."

Further down the hall, about thirty people manned computer terminals in the Research Division. Denton introduced the reporters to Farley Johnson, who had just found another database full of names to merge with Eulenco's bulging database.

"Computers have transformed politics in America," Johnson said. "We feed in tons of demographic data and the mainframes organize it. They allow our Marketing Division to target direct mailings very precisely to specific age and interest groups, with messages slanted to address issues of concern to the specific groups."

In the Advertising Division, film editors merged video clips and computer graphics into television commercials while media buyers worked the phones, closing deals for last-minute newspaper ads and precious air time on television and radio stations.

"What do you mean it's not nasty enough?" an advertising copywriter demanded of a Jerome adviser. *"We're calling the governor a crook, an embezzler and a liar—and it's only a thirty-second spot!"*

Denton excused himself to make a telephone call. An Ad Division employee invited Marilyn and McGraw to view a series of thirty-second spots. One of them paired a photo of Governor Dodge with a shot of a rotting Chicago slum. Trash littered the streets, houses were falling apart, and two black actors playing the roles of drug dealer and junky could be seen making a deal.

"Have you had enough of Governor Dodge's liberal policies?" asked an announcer with a deep voice. "So have we!"

From a glass-enclosed office inside the Ad Division, Denton kept a close eye on Marilyn and McGraw as he called his security chief.

"Call off your hounds, Moss. The two reporters are at Eulenco. Tell Randall to tail them when they leave."

"No can do. Randall won't be back from California till tomorrow. I'll send Wolfman."

"Wolfman? He made it back from San Francisco?"

"Yeah. He was banged up by the fall into the swimming pool, but he eluded the cops."

"Make sure he does what he's told this time! Tell him to follow the reporters and, when he gets the chance, snatch copies of German newspapers reporting Harry's death. Get those and any other photos and documents the reporters have."

"Wolfman probably would knock off the reporters for free. He's pissed at 'em."

"*No!* We can control this. The reporters want to meet with Harry. If Harry does his part, we'll come out of this smelling like a rose. ... Tell Wolfman I'll keep the reporters here for a half hour or so."

Down another wood-paneled hallway, Eulenco employees prepared targeted direct mail literature in the Marketing Division. Some of the mailings promoted Jerome's candidacy. McGraw suspected other mailings—designed to give the impression they had been mailed by Governor Dodge's supporters—were calculated to offend and anger those who received them.

Across the hall in the Polling Division, a dozen experienced pollsters structured new polls or tabulated results from surveys already concluded.

"We conduct the most extensive polls in the state on candidates and issues," Denton said. "We can identify and respond to shifts in voter attitude very quickly."

Tucked away in a far corner of the Eulenco building was the Communications Room, which housed forty television monitors and a vast array of radio-receiving equipment.

"Television and radio stations and newspapers from around the state are monitored around-the-clock," Denton noted.

"The C.I.A. would call this an intelligence-gathering operation," McGraw suggested.

"Nonsense. It is nothing of the sort. We track media coverage of the campaign. Other campaigns do it. We simply do it more efficiently."

In Eulenco's basement, Denton led the reporters to another area that housed expensive-looking computer terminals and equipment. Lettering on the door announced it was the "SIMULATIONS DIVISION".

"This is where highly skilled technicians run simulations of possible scenarios as campaign developments unfold. We feed in data about the candidates' schedules, their stands on the issues, news developments and poll results. The computers extrapolate from the data all likely consequences. These scenarios reduce the element of surprise and allow us to alter the course of the election in the direction we wish to see it unfold."

"I bet you didn't count on us barging into your office saying your candidate is dead," McGraw suggested.

Denton smiled. That was exactly what he had expected McGraw and Marilyn to do. "No, that comes under the heading of 'Campaign Developments Too Absurd To Foresee'. ... Thanks to the simulations, we don't waste all our time reacting to day-by-day developments. We're more concerned with what will happen over the longer haul. ... Do either of you play chess?"

McGraw and Marilyn said they did not.

"Great chess players think several moves into the future. If your queen takes your opponent's bishop now, will your queen be vulnerable six moves down the road? Well, we're doing the same thing with election strategy. Before we make a move, we explore on a computer all foreseeable possible consequences."

Denton led the way to an elevator and they returned to the lobby on the first floor. "Well, that's the grand tour. A parting word: stop circulating absurd allegations. Jerome will straighten everything out when you talk to him."

"When will that be?" McGraw demanded. "We aren't going to wait forever."

"Of course not." Denton pulled out a book listing Harry's campaign appearances. "Hmm ... I tell you what. In two days, he'll launch a series of major campaign appearances in the Chicago area. He's speaking at the Woodfield Mall in Schaumburg on Saturday. You can meet with him afterwards. Ask him anything you want. It should settle this once and for all. Fair enough?"

"It sounds fair," Marilyn conceded.

"Remember what I said about watching your step. You're on very slippery ice."

As McGraw departed from the Eulenco building with Marilyn, he realized the shabby building housing the Jerome Campaign Headquarters in Peoria symbolized the old, street-corner politics. The futuristic Eulenco building represented the new politics, dominated by computers and television.

"Something tells me that two or three moves into the future, the computer will tell Murray to get rid of us," McGraw said. "I didn't like the way he said Chicago would settle things 'once and for all'."

"You're getting paranoid, McGraw. They wouldn't try anything at a crowded shopping mall."

McGraw and Marilyn cruised east on Sangamon Avenue in the Buick. They didn't notice Wolfman tailing them in a gray Chrysler PT Cruiser.

Wolfman called Moss on his cell phone. "Can I whack the reporters?"

"Negative. Denton wants you to retrieve all their papers, notes and photos. That's it."

"He still doesn't get it. Just remember: when he wants them whacked, I want to do it!"

"Your request is noted, Wolfgang. Now take your anger level down a few notches and follow orders!"

Moss hung up.

"And *you* are next on my list," Wolfgang mumbled.

Marilyn and McGraw returned to the Middle Western Motel and an hour later drove to a Hardee's down the street, where they ordered hamburgers and fries.

While the reporters were gone, Wolfman wandered into the Middle Western Motel. Still tired and irritable after the debacle at the Bay Vista Hotel, he was in no mood to spar with Maude Waddel.

"What do you need?" Maude growled.

Randall fished out a photo of McGraw and Marilyn taken by a security camera at Eulenco.

"You seen these two?" he asked.

"Sure! Guy named Slater and his wife!"

"What room are they in?"

Maude didn't like the looks of the visitor. He reminded her of her first husband. "Don't think they're in their room. Saw 'em leave a few minutes ago."

Randall moved closer and glared.

"What room?"

"They expecting you?"

"Yes, ma'am. We're old friends. Slater and me did time together."

"One twenty two," said Maude.

As the stranger headed for room 122, Maude grumbled, "I gotta get a better clientele."

When McGraw and Marilyn returned to the motel a half hour later, they discovered their room had been ransacked. Someone had stolen McGraw's laptop computer and the photo, newspaper articles and notes they had accumulated.

"Now I'm angry!" McGraw grumbled, as he picked up a lamp that had been tossed on the floor.

"They obviously knew what they were looking for," Marilyn noted. "They didn't take anything else."

"Have any friends who might give us a place to stay?"

"Maybe. Ann Pageant, a Channel 10 reporter, just moved to a new condo and she's trying to sublet her old apartment. She might let us use it."

"Tell her we don't need much," McGraw said. "Three or four bedrooms, living room with a cathedral ceiling, kitchen with a full refrigerator, hot tub and, oh, yes, tennis courts."

Marilyn ignored McGraw as she called Ann at the station.

"A Chicago reporter and I need a place to hang out for a few days, Ann. Could we use your old apartment?"

"Ohhhh. You found a live one, Marilyn?"

"Not really. We're working on a story together. Strictly business and strictly confidential."

McGraw stopped straightening up the room long enough to glare at Marilyn. "Strictly business? I give you my best and it's 'strictly business'? We're going to have a serious talk in bed tonight."

Marilyn covered up the receiver. "McGraw, will you shut up?" She uncovered it. "Yes, that was him. ... Yes, well, he's starved for sex and it's affected his mind. So can we use your apartment?"

"Well, sure. Stop by the station and I'll give you the key."

"Ask her what's in the refrigerator," McGraw insisted.

Marilyn sighed. "McGraw wants to know what's in the refrigerator"

"Probably some wilted lettuce. You might want to pick up some food."

As Marilyn hung up, McGraw was mumbling: "Starved for sex ... affected my mind ... "

"Stop your griping. We've got an apartment!"

The reporters threw their things into the Buick. Marilyn drove her Mustang to the television station to pick up the apartment keys, taking a circuitous route to prevent anyone from following her. McGraw drove to a Best Buy store, where he bought a Compaq laptop computer, and then headed to a Kroger's grocery store where he loaded up on sirloin, beer, frozen pizza, lettuce, bread and eggs. The lettuce and eggs were for Marilyn.

They rendezvoused at the red brick Regal Court Apartments complex on the west side of the city. Pageant's apartment had one bedroom, a living room and a small kitchen. As Marilyn slipped a frozen pizza in the oven, McGraw used the *Chronicle* credit card to call Hans Montag at the *Kurier-Presse* in Berlin.

"Herr McGraw! How are you?"

"Our motel room was burglarized and a few people probably want us dead. It hasn't been a good week."

"I envy you. You live an exciting life. ... uh ... Please wait a moment."

In the *Kurier-Presse* newsroom, Ernst Langer approached Hans holding a computer printout of a story.

"Hans, that mass murderer you interviewed a while back ... did he really threaten you?"

Hans shrugged. "He said he would tear my heart out and feed it to the lions at the zoo. I took it as a threat."

"I was just wondering," Langer said, as he started back to his desk. "An hour ago, a judge freed him because of a technicality."

"Terrific," Hans muttered.

"What is it?" McGraw asked. "What's wrong?"

"My week just took a turn for the worse, too."

"Could you do a big favor for me, Hans?"

"Jawohl ... I will be happy to take your girlfriend off your hands for a while."

"That's not the favor. Could you e-mail me another copy of the pages reporting that Harry and Nancy Jerome died in the car crash? The burglar took the copies I had."

"Certainly. I'll send them when I can."

"I appreciate it, Hans. But we need them *very soon!*"

"No problem. I understand. ... Herr McGraw, let me pose a *theoretische Frage* ... what do you call it? ... a hypothetical question."

'Sure.'

"Suppose you interviewed a mass murderer, and during the interview you called him things like road kill and toilet breath, and he seemed a little upset about it, and then let's say that he was set free."

"I suppose I would take a hypothetical vacation for a couple weeks."

"Uh, huh. A vacation."

"But I would do it *after* I sent the stories to my pal in America."

"Of course."

25

4 days before the election

As Marilyn rustled up eggs and toast at Ann Pageant's apartment, McGraw watched the news on Channel 10 ...

"While Governor Dodge campaigns in Rockford today, his opponent in the fall election, Harry Jerome, is in Champaign, where he will tell University of Illinois alumni about his gridiron adventures at San Jose State University in the early Sixties."

"Red Grange was known at the 'galloping ghost' when he played at Illinois," McGraw pointed out. "Maybe that's what they should call Jerome."

"In other news, Chicago-based Hudson Communications announced this morning it will sell two of its television stations and three newspapers in the Southeast to Bolton Media. It is an unusual move for Hudson, which increased its stable of media properties steadily in recent years. Analysts say Hudson is having cash flow problems and needs additional funds to back its bid for

Seven Moon Communications, a Singapore-based satellite television corporation."

Suddenly, someone knocked loudly at the door.

"Who is it?" McGraw asked warily.

"What difference does my name make? You don't know me."

McGraw opened the door wide enough to see a slender, tough-looking man, about six-feet tall with short black hair.

"What do you need?" McGraw asked.

"A decent haircut and a new car. What do you need?"

McGraw let the stranger in. "How about answering my questions?"

The man nodded at Marilyn and plopped into a chair. "I've seen you two around. You're the only reporters who seem interested in what's really going on in Jerome's campaign."

"What do you know about it?" Marilyn asked.

"I've been doing a little poking around myself. I'm Nick Burnbaum. When Harry got shot a few months ago, I was the Chicago cop assigned to the case. When I started asking questions, someone turned up the heat on my superiors and I was told to lay off. Harry had become a hero and someone didn't want me digging any deeper into it."

"There was more to the shooting?" Marilyn asked. "I thought it was cut-and-dried."

"There was more to it."

"Like what?" McGraw said, as he handed Burnbaum a cup of coffee.

The detective grimaced. "You can't quote me or use me as a source. You must confirm everything yourself. ... It became obvious this wasn't just another convenience store robbery that Harry happened to break up. Some things didn't add up ... Peter Lorton wasn't the holdup man's real name. It was Peter Solado. The day before the robbery, sixty grand was deposited into a checking account with Solado's name on it. So I asked myself why would Solado hold up a convenience store if he didn't need the cash? And where did he get the sixty grand?"

"Come up with any answers?"

"I'm working on it. Someone is covering their tracks well. ... I don't like being told to lay off cases. I don't care who is involved. I want you to nail Jerome, but I've gotta be careful what I tell you. If it's traced to me, I'll be directing traffic on State Street 'til the end of time." Burnbaum got up. "It can get damn cold on State Street. ... You only have a few days before the election. You've got a lot of work to do." As he reached the door, he turned. "By the way, I'm sure you talked to Mrs. Searcy. Isn't she a nice lady!"

McGraw and Marilyn watched through the window as Burnbaum headed for the parking lot.

"Who is Mrs. Searcy?" McGraw asked. It was obvious Burnbaum was telling McGraw and Marilyn they *should* talk to her.

"Searcy ... He was that Eulenco employee killed in a plane crash!" Marilyn exclaimed.

"That's it! Maybe Slater was right. He said from the start there was something fishy about that crash. It's possible Searcy was on to something and Harry's people had him killed."

The telephone book listed an address for Morton Searcy on West Lawrence Street.

Later that morning, McGraw and Marilyn pulled up in front of the wood frame house. A large oak tree cast a shadow over most of the front yard. A '78 Ford sat in the driveway.

A brick sidewalk led to a front porch which needed a paint job. No one had bothered to fetch the morning newspaper.

Marilyn knocked on the front door. Moments later, a brunette who seemed to be in her mid-fifties opened the door enough to see who was there.

"Yes?"

"Mrs. Searcy?"

The woman did not respond.

"Mrs. Searcy, I'm Marilyn Westley of Channel 10 and this is David McGraw, a *Chicago Chronicle* reporter. We'd like to talk to you about your husband."

"Don't have time to talk."

The door began to close.

"Wait!" Marilyn said. "Mrs. Searcy, you don't need to be afraid of us. We just want to find out more about how your husband died."

The woman looked them over. Her eyes had a vacant look, as though something inside her had died when Morton's body was found.

"How do I know you really are reporters?"

Marilyn and McGraw rifled through their clothing looking for press cards.

"I'm sure I've got it," Marilyn said.

McGraw had no luck rummaging through his billfold. "Haven't used the thing in ages," he grumbled.

They showed the woman their driver's licenses.

"I reckon you can come in. If you were pretending to be reporters, you'd try to look like you knew what you were doing."

"Have we been insulted?" McGraw asked, as Searcy's widow led them into the living room.

"I'm not sure," Marilyn said.

The house was small but clean, and everything was in

its place. Mrs. Searcy sat in a brown vinyl rocking chair, Marilyn and McGraw on the sofa. They quickly discovered it was one of those soft sofas that made you feel like you were sitting on a large marshmallow.

"Don't know if I should talk to you," the widow said. "Maybe someone sent you to find out if I know anything."

"About your husband's death?" McGraw asked. "Do you know anything about it?"

She sighed. "You see, Morton was always an honest person. He took a job at Eulenco last year because the job paid good. At first, he enjoyed his work. Later, he became more unhappy, and I could tell he was worried. He noticed a lot of things he didn't agree with, and he'd tell me he was getting in deeper and deeper. Didn't say what was going on 'cause he didn't want to worry me or put me in danger. I kept telling him—if it bothers you that much, get out of there. Quit—it's only a job. He said he didn't know if he *could* quit. Didn't know if they'd let him."

"He didn't say *anything* about what was going on?"

"No. I'm sorry."

McGraw leaned forward. "Did he give you any papers to keep for him? Or was there someplace he could have stashed information he didn't want anyone to see?"

"I haven't found any papers. Someone broke into the house a few days after Morton died. Maybe they took them … I don't think Morton gave anything like that to Gary."

"Who's Gary?" McGraw asked.

"Gary Fletcher. A young man who works at Eulenco. My husband said Gary was the only one at Eulenco he trusted— the only one who wasn't sucked in by it all. But I don't know if Gary will talk to you."

McGraw and Marilyn conversed with Mrs. Searcy for

several more minutes, but they knew what their next move would be.

They said goodbye to Mrs. Searcy. As they made their way to the front door, Marilyn noticed photographs hanging on a living room wall. One showed Searcy and another young man in college football uniforms.

"May I borrow this picture?" Marilyn asked.

"Sure," Mrs. Searcy said. "That's Morton and his college roommate."

"San Jose State?"

"Yes."

"Do you remember his roommate's name?"

"No. I'm sorry."

"C'mon, Marilyn," McGraw called from the front porch. "Let's go!"

"What's that?" McGraw asked, as he drove back to the apartment.

"Picture of Searcy. He played football at San Jose State. The other player is his roommate—and I think it's Harry Jerome!"

"Wow! We'll check it out. Good work, kid."

"Gee, thanks, dad."

"We've got to be careful with Fletcher," McGraw warned. "We don't want to scare him off. If Harry's people killed Searcy they wouldn't hesitate to kill Fletcher—or us."

"Well, Fletcher is a man. Obviously, *I* should be the one to make contact."

McGraw eyed her warily. "What kind of contact?"

"I'll call him at work. Set up a date. Flirt a little. Make him feel comfortable with me. Then he'll spill his guts."

They drove along for a few blocks in silence.

"Nice of you to offer to make the sacrifice, but I don't think that's a good idea," McGraw said.

"Why not?"

"There might be another way ... something less painful for Fletcher."

"You're jealous! McGraw, there's nothing to worry about. I'll be very careful, and you'll be nearby. Things won't get out of hand."

"Damn right they won't."

At the apartment, Marilyn called Eulenco and asked to speak to Gary Fletcher. The operator rang an extension.

"This is Gary."

"Hi, Gary. This is Marilyn Westley. I'm a reporter for Channel 10."

"I know. We already met."

"We did?" She covered up the phone. "He says we met! He knows who I am!"

McGraw grimaced. "We're dead. If he met you, he'll never agree to go out with you."

Marilyn pushed McGraw off the bed.

"I'm glad you remember me, Gary."

"I didn't think you'd be calling me. Is that other reporter with you?"

Marilyn covered up the phone again. "He knows you, too! How does he know us?"

"I don't know anyone from Eulenco but Denton," McGraw said. "And there was that long-hair in Peoria who gave us the low-down on Harry's California trip."

"That's it!" Marilyn said. *"That was Gary Fletcher!"* She uncovered the phone. "No, the other reporter isn't with me. I don't run into him very often. He's not my type."

"I don't have to take this," McGraw grumbled, as Marilyn put her hand over the phone again. "There's this girl Maria, back in Chicago. She's crazy about me."

"Shut up, McGraw!"

Fletcher asked, "How did you happen to call me?"

"I know someone in personnel at Eulenco. She gave me your name. I thought we might go out together sometime, if you're free."

"A date? Well, sure! It's hard to believe your dating book isn't filled every night. How would you like to go to a country-western bar with me tomorrow night?"

Marilyn hated country and western bars. "I'd love to! But we'll need to make it for Monday. I'm going up to Chicago for a couple days. How about noon on Monday?"

"That'll be fine. Should I pick you up?"

"I'll meet you there."

"All right. The Tombstone Bar on Adams Street. See you Monday."

VI

Confrontation
in Chicago

26

By 8 A.M., Marilyn and McGraw were cruising along Interstate 55, bound for Chicago in the *Chronicle*'s Buick.

"Relax," Marilyn said, as McGraw forced a Datsun off the road. "We're finally going to get our interview with Harry."

"Why do I have the feeling Murray Denton has his fishing rod out and we're the catch of the day?"

"You think it's a trap? They wouldn't try to get rid of us when so many people are around."

"Who knows what they'd do—particularly if they see we're trying to get his fingerprints. They're desperate."

By the time Marilyn and McGraw reached Joliet, they had run out of things to say. The car radio intruded on their thoughts … Dionne Warwick warbling that she'd never fall in love again. It was followed by the news:

"With three days to go before the election, the race for governor is heating up. The Chicago Sentinel *reported this morning that Governor Stephen Dodge had an affair with a female aide for two years after he took over the governor's office. Kathleen Nordstrom, who will appear Monday on television talk shows, told the* Sentinel *she made love to Dodge in the governor's office 'twenty or thirty times'. Governor Dodge's office called the allegations 'outrageous' and 'fabricated'. A spokesman for Harry Jerome said his organization had nothing to do with circulating the allegations, but added the reports 'clearly demonstrate the need for a new governor with higher moral and ethical standards'."*

Traffic clogged the Adlai E. Stevenson Expressway as McGraw and Marilyn arrived in the Windy City later that morning. McGraw served as Marilyn's guide. She had seen Chicago many times, but never with him. The towering skyscrapers contrasted sharply with Springfield's modest commercial buildings.

"No one knows how many people live in their cars," McGraw said. "Some are homeless. Others have been looking for a parking place so long they qualify as homeless."

"I don't believe you, McGraw."

From the expressway, they could see a police SWAT team raiding an old apartment house.

"I lived in those apartments five or six years ago," McGraw said. "They've fixed them up a little."

In the distance, fire devoured a grocery store.

"Looks like they'll be selling ice cream and milk cheap tonight."

"Why does anyone live here, McGraw? It's so crowded."

"Are you kidding? We've got the Bulls, Bears, White Sox, Cubs, Black Hawks and great sports bars."

"Everything modern civilization requires."

"Exactly!"

Just ahead on the expressway loomed a sign: "Construction Next Five Miles."

Marilyn and McGraw checked into the Park Hyatt Hotel on Water Tower Square, a luxurious hotel on the Magnificent Mile, not far from Lake Michigan. Slater would have suggested a Motel 6 or a Budget Inn, but McGraw figured the *Chronicle* could afford more extravagant accommodations.

After they settled into their room, McGraw called Slater and arranged to meet him that afternoon at Morelli's.

Pete Morelli greeted McGraw and Marilyn shortly before 3 P.M. and led them to a table near the front window.

"Where did McGraw find a woman willing to go out with him?" Morelli wondered aloud.

"We're reporters, working on a story," Marilyn explained.

"Oh, I understand. I wasn't goin' to serve you on account of if you date McGraw, you must have really low standards, but since everything is on the up and up, what would you like?"

"Less conversation," McGraw suggested.

Marilyn ordered the ravioli, McGraw the spaghetti and meatballs.

A few moments later, Maria hustled out of the kitchen carrying baskets of Italian bread.

"McGraw!"

"Hi, Maria. This is Marilyn."

"You're hanging out with McGraw?" Maria asked her. "Are things that bad out there?"

"It's a dating jungle."

"I hear you, honey. I've dated a few animals, too."

"Pipe down, Maria," McGraw said. "Someone might think you're serious."

Marilyn laughed as Maria returned to the kitchen. "So that's Maria ... the one who's crazy about you?"

"I meant to say she's just plain crazy."

Slater arrived, looking harried as usual, as though he were a few heartbeats away from a cardiac event.

McGraw introduced Marilyn to Slater and explained that the attractive young television reporter was helping him track down the Jerome story.

"I've heard a lot about you," Marilyn said. "You don't look like a vampire."

"First I've heard about you, but I knew something was up when I got my credit card bill. Did you visit San Francisco recently—at the *Chronicle*'s expense?"

McGraw shifted in his chair uneasily. "Uh ... let's stick to the matter at hand."

Slater told Maria he wanted the lasagna. She returned to the table with lettuce salads for all of them.

"The problem," McGraw said, "is that we only have three days to wrap up the rest of the story."

"Less than that," Slater said. "I'll need it Monday evening. But you've got the story, right? All you're lacking is a few details?"

"Right. A few little things ... proof that Harry died, the identity of the surrogate running for governor, the names of people behind the conspiracy and why they're doing it."

"*I knew it! You don't have the story!* Why did I bring you back from that rag in Florida? You've been screwing around with UFOs and Bigfoot so long you've forgotten what reporting is!"

"Slater, we'll get the story. The computer with the files showing how German papers reported Harry's death was stolen, but my contact in Germany is e-mailing the graphics to me again. I'll send you a copy of the computer files and you can have them translated. That will prove Harry Jerome died sixteen years ago in a car crash. Tonight, we have an interview set up with Jerome at the Woodfield Mall in Schaumburg, and while I'm putting the fear of God in him, Marilyn will get his fingerprints. The prints should either prove he's Harry Jerome or tell us who the hell he is—if the prints are on file somewhere. And, we'll get the rest of the story when we return to Springfield and confront Gary Fletcher, Morton Searcy's buddy. Searcy was the Eulenco employee killed in the plane crash."

"Right. I remember," Slater said. "For your sake, let's hope Fletcher knows what's going on. What's your backup plan if you can't get Harry's prints and Fletcher doesn't know anything?"

McGraw sighed. "I suppose we'd break into Eulenco, the consulting firm running the campaign. Murray Denton is bound to have incriminating papers lying around."

"McGraw, you can't even get past security at the *Chronicle*—and you work there. There's no way you're going to break into Eulenco."

Maria served their lasagna, ravioli and spaghetti. Morelli refilled their wine glasses.

"It's hard to believe anyone would be brazen enough to run a surrogate candidate for governor," Slater suggested.

"Depends how badly they want power," McGraw said. "I think a few powerful people in the state were desperate to find an electable candidate to defeat Governor Dodge, so they created one—and gave him the name of a California man who died sixteen years ago because they wanted to use Harry Jerome's background. They tried to destroy all the records of his death, and they didn't count on anyone finding out he had a son. All they had to do was find someone to play the role of 'candidate Harry Jerome'. They could mold the candidate into anything they wanted him to be. After Harry's elected, his backers will control the state government."

"But *why* do they want to control state government?" Slater asked.

"We haven't figured that out yet," McGraw admitted.

"Boggles the mind how they expect to pull it off," Slater mumbled.

"They know that style and image count for more than substance," Marilyn said. "Harry's backers are swamping voters with propaganda, targeted mailings and misleading television ads. Voters don't know what's real and what isn't."

McGraw nodded. "Most people never see candidates or celebrities except on TV. They accept their existence as fact because the media tell them these people exist."

Slater leaned back in his chair and considered what the reporters had told him. "Without proof, you've got nothing."

McGraw wiped spaghetti off his chin. "Even if we don't nail down the rest of the story before the election, we can tell people a dead man's running for governor."

Slater grimaced. "I don't think so. Jerome's people would deny it, and we'd look like fools if we say Harry died sixteen years ago but can't tell people *who* the new Jerome is, *who*'s backing him and *why* they're running a dead man for governor. We can't do this half-assed. There's too much at stake. If you're wrong or we botch the story, there will be huge libel suits, the *Chronicle*'s reputation will be destroyed, and we'll all lose our jobs. ... Things were a lot less complicated when Carl Yorbly sent me PR handouts about Jerome every day." Slater got up from the table. "Well, it's been real. You've got a helluva lot of work to do. And if you commit any felonies, I'll deny I ever heard of you."

"Actually, Slater, I was thinking you might help us."

Slater shook his head. "Sorry. Criminal activities aren't part of my job description." He glanced at his watch. "Oh-oh. Gotta get back to the office. Need to remind some copyeditors and reporters who's boss. Call me later."

27

The huge Woodfield Mall housed about three hundred stores and restaurants. When Harry Jerome arrived in a chauffeur-driven Cadillac shortly before 7 P.M. that Saturday evening, he was the picture of confidence and trustworthiness. Television and newspaper reporters shouted questions to Jerome as cameramen recorded his arrival. McGraw and Marilyn hovered in the background.

Duncan Jamieson, Roger Moss and a half dozen other aides and security men rushed Jerome inside the mall.

A half hour later, Jerome could be seen in a roped-off area eighty feet from a podium which had been erected for the occasion. More than five thousand people had gathered to hear the candidate. A huge screen—the type found in ballparks and auditoriums—loomed behind the podium.

Lance Reynolds, a Chicago-area congressman, introduced Jerome, hailing him as the candidate who could bring Illinois out of its doldrums and lead the state to prosperity.

Hearty applause welcomed Jerome as he made his way to the podium. The candidate smiled broadly and waved to the crowd. Shouts of "Harry! Harry!" erupted. Jerome let the groundswell build. When it slackened, he fished a stack of notes from his pocket.

"My wife Nancy, who died sixteen years ago, bless her soul, loved to shop. I'm not sure if she went to Heaven or if she's spending eternity at the Woodfield Mall, but I can assure you she's happy in either case."

Appreciative laughter swept the mall. Jerome could be a charmer.

"It's a tribute to the good, old-fashioned thriftiness of people like you that you still have money to spend at malls after the way Dodge has been taxing the life out of you!"

Applause greeted his remark.

"The great state of Illinois has no problems that can't be solved. And the problems can be solved without raising taxes! When I am governor, there will be no new taxes—and I will cut state income taxes!"

Still more applause.

"The private sector is the key!" Jerome insisted. *"Efficiency in private enterprises and incentives for business will do more for the people of Illinois than raising taxes and increasing spending on social programs!"*

On the big screen, McGraw could see beads of sweat rolling down Jerome's forehead. He was working the crowd like an evangelist, aiming not at the intellect but at the emotions. He was stirring up The Faithful so they would battle for The Cause.

"Remember what John F. Kennedy said ... 'The world is different now ... and yet the same revolutionary belief for which our forbears fought is still at issue around the globe, the belief that the

rights of man come not from the generosity of the state but from the hand of God.'"

Jerome turned his attention to another topic …

"Now, maybe you've noticed that some of the news media in this state haven't given me much coverage," he thundered, *"and when they do use something about me, it's usually wrong."*

McGraw flinched.

"The liberals who run the Chicago Chronicle *and most of the nation's newspapers and television stations don't want you to know the truth. They circulate rumors and lies about our campaign. But I'll tell you something—it won't matter because we will win anyway!"*

Cheering greeted Jerome's declarations.

McGraw shook his head. "Most of the coverage of Harry's campaign comes from Harry's press releases!" he told Marilyn.

"And the truth is, this state of ours—like the country itself—is in a heap of trouble. Crime is rampant, the flow of drugs can't be stemmed, immorality abounds. But my opponent doesn't want to deal with these problems. He's more concerned with pushing the state further into debt and giving people with unusual sexual orientations special protection under the law. Too bad he doesn't give that much attention to the common people who struggle to eke out a living every day."

Shouts of "Down with Dodge!" filled the mall. Jerome beamed. He seemed to gain strength from the emotional fervor he was whipping up.

As Jerome wound down his oratory, Marilyn and McGraw pushed closer to the stage. Jerome signed autographs as a security man guided him toward an empty store in the mall that had been set up for use by Jerome and his people. The two reporters followed.

McGraw called out to him: "Mr. Jerome! David McGraw of the *Chronicle*. Marilyn Westley and I have an appointment to interview you."

Jerome stopped and faced the reporters. "Yes. You have come to interview the dead man." He smiled at his little joke.

The reporters followed the candidate, Press Secretary Jamieson, Roger Moss and the security detail into the vacant store, where a table and a few folding chairs had been set up. As Marilyn passed in front of Jerome, she dropped a notebook with a plastic cover. Jerome picked it up and handed it to her. She handled it carefully.

The two reporters sat on one side of the table while Jerome, Jamieson and Moss seated themselves on the other.

"Who are you?" McGraw asked.

"Harry Ashley Jerome."

"No you're not. Harry Jerome is dead. And for your part in this charade, you could spend the rest of your life in jail. Your only hope is to tell us who's behind this."

Jerome seemed stunned by the onslaught.

"That's absurd!" declared Jamieson.

"Then how do you account for the fact that Harry Jerome died in an automobile crash sixteen years ago on an autobahn outside Berlin."

"But I didn't," Jerome insisted. "I hear you referred to newspaper articles that reported my death as well as my wife's. May I see those articles?"

"I don't have them. But I did have them. And Marilyn saw them, too. They were stolen. I'll soon have new copies."

Jamieson handed Jerome a brief case. Jerome pulled a piece of paper out of it.

"This is how my hometown paper, the *Ukiah Standard*, reported the accident."

McGraw and Marilyn read the lead headline:

CRASH IN WEST GERMANY
KILLS UKIAH RESIDENT

Nancy Jerome Mourned;
Husband Harry Recovering

McGraw and Marilyn examined the paper. It was a pho-
tocopy. They suspected the original used to make the copy
was not genuine. The type was too sharp and clear for a
newspaper page more than twenty years old. Someone had
gone to a lot of trouble to produce the page, but the effort
was not convincing.

"You see, you were mistaken," Jerome said. "I am will-
ing to assume it was an honest mistake."

"But I saw copies of stories from two German papers
that reported the crash also killed Harry Jerome!" McGraw
insisted.

"I believe I know what happened," Harry said. "As the
Ukiah story states, first reports said that both my wife and
I had died. Police later issued a clarification noting that my
wife had died and I was in the hospital. The West German
papers obviously went to press before the clarification was
issued."

McGraw was taken aback. It was an ingenious explanation—and it was the denial Slater expected. But McGraw
was not about to take the explanation at face value. The
Jerome campaign had floated too many lies and half-truths
in the campaign. Since Harry and his people were not backing down, the fingerprints were even more important now.

"Why all the secrecy in your campaign?" Marilyn asked.
"Why have you been hiding from the press?"

"My dear young lady, I haven't been hiding. I simply have not been answering reporters' questions after my appearances."

"Why don't your press releases mention that you have a son?" asked Marilyn.

"He has a right to privacy," Harry said.

Jamieson rose to his feet. "I'm afraid that's all the time we have. I hope Mr. Jerome answered your questions."

"You won't get away with it," McGraw warned Harry.

Roger Moss noticed Marilyn wasn't using the notebook Harry had picked up. She had put it in a plastic bag and was treating it gingerly. He realized it had Harry's fingerprints on it.

"It looks like your notebook is damaged," Moss said, as he reached for it. "Let us give you another one."

Marilyn held the notebook out of reach. "Not on your life!"

"Get the notebook!" Moss ordered.

McGraw and Marilyn burst out of the room.

"Stop those two!" Moss told the security detail.

Marilyn and McGraw raced through the crowded mall. Moss and the security crew scurried after them, trying to keep them in sight. With so many shoppers bobbing around, it was not easy.

The reporters ducked inside Macy's and waited to see if the security men spotted them. Harry's men were still on their trail. Marilyn and McGraw joined a group of nursing home residents who were moving in the opposite direction, back toward the security men. As the security men hunted for the reporters, Moss scrutinized the seniors. He couldn't see the faces of those farthest from him. He moved closer.

Suddenly, he spotted Marilyn and McGraw, crouched down low in the middle of the group.

"There they are!"

Marilyn and McGraw took off running with the security guards in pursuit. Marilyn bumped into a senior citizen and the notebook sailed into the air. McGraw scooped it up and kept on running.

Moss shoved some of the shoppers out of the way. A few fell to the ground. The security guards hurdled them.

"What the hell is going on?" demanded one middle-aged man who had been shoved to the ground.

"Must be a sale somewhere," suggested his wife.

The reporters ran out of the mall and down the street, dodging cars, until they came to a Chevy Malibu and jumped in.

The driver shook his head. "I can't believe I'm driving a getaway car," he moaned.

It was Slater.

"Get moving, Slater!"

Marilyn and McGraw ducked down in the back seat as Slater hit the gas. The Malibu lurched forward.

"Did you get Harry's prints?" the state editor asked.

"We got them," Marilyn said.

"Good. I'd hate to think I was committing a felony for nothing. … If they really are Harry Jerome's prints, you've got a lot to answer for!"

"If they were Harry's prints, they wouldn't have any reason to chase us," McGraw pointed out. "Get us out of here!"

The brakes of the Malibu screeched as it rounded a corner. Slater relaxed when he saw that no one was following them.

"I could do this," he said. "I could drive getaway cars. Don't know why people think it's so hard."

Suddenly a car carrying Roger Moss and two security men shot out from a side street, forcing Slater to do a 180-degree turn. He raced back the way he had come.

McGraw realized Slater was about to run a red light and have a close encounter with a fire truck.

"Look out!"

Somehow, Slater managed to just miss the fire truck.

"Now you see why I don't drive in Chicago traffic," Slater muttered. "That, and the fact they took away my license."

"Oh, Lord," Marilyn moaned.

"At least the cops won't be chasing us," McGraw noted. "Only the campaign's security crew. Denton wouldn't want to get the police involved."

Slater whipped the Malibu into a parking garage. The three of them waited as the security men sped by.

"This has not been one of my favorite days," Slater said.

Back at the Park Hyatt Hotel, McGraw couldn't reach Nick Burnbaum—he was still in central Illinois—so he called another Chicago cop, Burt Reardon.

"I need a big favor, Burt. We've got fingerprints on a notebook. Can you run a make on them for me?"

"McGraw, this is the police department, not a drive-through for reporters who want to play cop."

"I need your help, Reardon! I wouldn't ask if it wasn't important!"

"All right. Don't blow a gasket. But don't come around here. Meet me at 9 tomorrow morning in Grant Park, near Buckingham Fountain."

28

Sunday, November 5

2 days before the election

After breakfast in the Park Hyatt's dazzling NoMI restaurant, McGraw drove Marilyn to Grant Park. They had no trouble finding Buckingham Fountain, but Reardon was not there. They waited on a bench near the fountain as a relentless breeze chilled them to the bone.

A few minutes after nine, Reardon arrived. He was walking a collie.

"Didn't know you had a dog," McGraw said.

"I don't. Borrowed it from a neighbor. Thought I'd look less conspicuous. Gotta get it back before the neighbor misses it."

"You stole a dog?"

"You aren't listening, McGraw. I said I borrowed it." Reardon gave Marilyn an approving glance from head to foot. "Your taste in women has improved, McGraw. I'll bet this is one girlfriend I won't have to bust for soliciting."

"Watch your language, Burt," McGraw grumbled. "Marilyn, this is Reardon. He's been defleaed, but he's not housebroken."

"Pleased to meet you, Marilyn. What's a fine looking woman like you doin' hangin' out with McGraw?"

"Everyone asks me that."

McGraw handed Reardon the cellophane bag containing the notebook. "Can you lift the fingerprints off this and run them?"

"Whose prints do you think they are?"

"I don't have any idea. And I don't want to tell you where we got them. But it's very important."

"All right. I'll do it as a favor for Marilyn."

Marilyn smiled. "Why, Patrolman Reardon. That's sweet."

Reardon took her right hand and kissed it. "It's nothin' darlin'. It comes naturally."

"So does horse manure," said McGraw.

"Keep a civil tongue when you're talkin' to the cops," Reardon said. "I'll call you in a couple days to let you know on the prints."

"Not good enough!" McGraw insisted. "We need it fast, Burt! This is an emergency!"

"All right." The collie jerked on the leash, letting Reardon know it wanted to leave. "You owe me big time, McGraw!"

McGraw called Slater to tell him they were leaving for Springfield.

"Be careful," Slater warned. "Jerome and his gang will probably stake out Channel 10 and other locations looking for you."

The reporters reluctantly checked out of the Park Hyatt

Hotel and by noon were cruising south on Interstate 55 in the general direction of Springfield.

Leaves already had fallen off some of the trees—a harbinger of winter and the snowy days ahead.

"Don't you just love cool days?" Marilyn mused.

She looked fetching in her fur-lined hooded jacket. Her cheeks were flush and her eyes sparkled. For her, McGraw might learn to tolerate winter. If he could tolerate her.

He switched on the radio. After three minutes of rap lyrics that seemed like three hours, the news came on.

"With only one day remaining before the election, Harry Jerome has taken the lead for the first time in the Chicago Star's *statewide poll. Jerome leads by only two percentage points over Governor Dodge, 46 to 44. The margin of error is three percent, so the race is virtually a dead heat. Jerome's gain in the polls comes on the heels of revelations about Governor Dodge's alleged affair with a woman who works in his office. Analysts agree the pressure is on Governor Dodge. Jerome has all the momentum, and he's planning a celebrity-studded Election Eve rally tomorrow night in Chicago that will be televised throughout the state."*

McGraw drove on as they listened to music on the radio. More than three hours after leaving Chicago, they passed a "Springfield City Limits" sign.

29

At Ann Pageant's apartment later that afternoon, McGraw fired up his laptop computer and checked his e-mail. Nothing from Germany. What was the matter with Hans? They needed copies of the papers reporting Harry's death!

McGraw browsed through the *Springfield Sunday News* as Marilyn sipped coffee.

"Denton's people are nervous because things are unraveling," McGraw said. "You and I aren't the only ones in danger. Harry Jerome Junior's family and Albert Thatch, the Ukiah newspaper editor, might be."

McGraw plopped into a red vinyl armchair in the living room and asked a long distance operator for Thatch's telephone number. Two minutes later, Thatch was on the phone.

"Albert? This is McGraw."

"McGraw! What's going on?"

"We're still trying to make sense of this Jerome mess. Did you find Jerome Junior and his family?"

"No, they're still missing."

"Someone stole all the notes and photos from my visit to Ukiah. You could be in danger. Be careful!"

"I will. Sounds like you're tryin' to earn that big salary, McGraw."

"Tryin' to, Thatch. Tryin' to. You still working sixty hour weeks?"

"Eighty, thanks to a dumbass reporter from Chicago who has me lookin' all over town for a missing family."

"Hang in there, Thatch. Maybe someday you, too, can work for a big city rag."

"Why you lazy, good-for-nothin'—"

A few minutes after 7 P.M., the phone rang.

"Reardon?" McGraw asked.

"Right."

"What's the story?"

"I might be more cooperative if you put Marilyn on the phone."

"This isn't The Dating Game. What have you got?"

"Well, the computer ID'd the prints as belonging to Harry Ashley Jerome."

McGraw's heart sank. "What?"

"I'm not done, McGraw. I noticed the file had been updated recently. Most people probably wouldn't have spotted that. Well, anyway, I retrieved the earlier records that had been deleted, and what d'ya know ... the prints ain't Harry Jerome's."

"Whose are they?"

Reardon read the name on the computer printout. "Hersch. Joseph Matlin Hersch of Mesa, Arizona, a suburb of Phoenix. Spelled H-E-R-S-C-H. All I have is his address and Social Security number. I called the Mesa Police Department, but they didn't have anything on him."

"You're a genius, Burt!"

"Tell me somethin' I don't know. ... So, what's goin' on, McGraw?"

"I'll tell you when I know. ... By the way, Reardon. I ordered a set of Sue Ellen Jerrell's get-rich-quick tapes for you."

McGraw didn't mention he charged them to the *Chronicle*'s credit card.

"You're all right, McGraw. I take back some of the bad things I said about you."

"Some of them? Why not all of them?"

"It's only two hundred and forty nine bucks."

Reardon gave McGraw the address and Social Security number for Hersch and hung up.

Marilyn and McGraw pondered the latest development.

"Joseph Hersch for governor. Is that it?" Marilyn asked.

"That's the size of it."

"What do we know about Hersch?"

"Nothing yet. Slater can run it down from his end. And when the credit bureau office opens tomorrow morning, I'll get a report on Hersch. That should tell us something."

McGraw called Slater. "Got a pencil handy? ... The candidate's real name is Joseph Matlin Hersch. He's from Mesa, Arizona. Here's his address and Social Security number ..."

"You're sure?"

"No, Slater, I called because I like driving you crazy. Well, all right, I *do* like driving you crazy, but I'm sure about Hersch. Have someone check him out."

"All right. Where's the rest of the story? ... McGraw? ... Don't hang up on me, McGraw!"

VII

One Day to Go —
Hold the Front Page!

30

The ringing of his cell phone jolted McGraw awake early the next morning. He reached over Marilyn and picked up the phone.

"This had better be very important," he said.

"Have you got the story?"

It was Slater.

"What time is it?"

"Six-ten."

"In the morning?"

"Yes. In the morning. The election is *tomorrow!*"

"You are a very demented person."

McGraw hung up.

"Who was it?" Marilyn asked. "Your mother?"

"No. Yours."

Realizing it would be a make-or-break day for them, the reporters summoned all their energy to get out of bed.

McGraw fired up his new laptop and discovered Hans had e-mailed the Jerome accident newspaper pages again. He e-mailed copies of the files to Slater. Then he showered while Marilyn, wearing a pink silk robe, threw together a breakfast of eggs, bacon and toast.

McGraw picked at the food absentmindedly as he skimmed the *Springfield Morning News*. The front page carried a story describing preparations for Harry's Election Eve bash in Chicago that evening. Among celebrities who would appear with Harry, the article noted, were the mayor of Chicago, six congressmen, two Hollywood actors, Sue Ellen Jerrell, Richard Dunnington of the Farrell Foundation, and Rev. Lawrence Drury. The story mentioned that the Jerome campaign was rumored to be spending "nearly a million dollars" on his campaign finale, which Hudson Communications would feed live to television and radio stations throughout the state.

McGraw bit into the toast. It was stone cold and as hard as a table top. "How long ago did you make the toast?"

"About a half hour. Eat it. It'll make your jaws strong."

"I think I broke a tooth."

Marilyn sipped the coffee. It was cold. Maybe McGraw wouldn't notice.

He did.

He stabbed a slice of blackened bacon with a fork. It broke into pieces.

"No offense, Marilyn, but this breakfast sucks."

"Yesterday morning we ate in a luxurious Chicago restaurant. It's not fair to compare my cooking to theirs."

"I was comparing your cooking to the garbage can out back."

"Quit complaining, McGraw. I'm a career woman, not a cook."

She cleared the dishes off the table. "So, to wrap up the story by this evening, we need to find out more about Hersch and find proof of the conspiracy and names of the people involved."

"Uh-huh."

"I'm going back to bed."

"No, you aren't. We've got a lot of work to do."

A loud noise spooked them. Someone with a heavy hand had knocked on the front door.

McGraw opened it cautiously. It was Nick Burnbaum.

"You've been busy," Burnbaum noted. He pushed past McGraw and Marilyn and headed for the kitchen. "Am I in time for breakfast?"

"Oh, brother, are you in the wrong place," McGraw said.

As Marilyn prepared a plate for Burnbaum, McGraw told the detective they had discovered Jerome's true identity.

Burnbaum nodded. "Joseph Hersch. Mesa, Arizona."

McGraw grimaced. "You could have saved us a lot of trouble by telling us that."

"I didn't have the information until yesterday."

"What else do you know about him?"

"Nothing yet. I'm working on it."

"That doesn't help us," McGraw said. "We need proof of who's behind the conspiracy to elect Harry and we need it fast."

Burnbaum reached for the plate of eggs, toast and bacon Marilyn had prepared for him. "I don't have any more than you do. Suspicions. No proof. What's your next move?"

"Searcy's widow thought Gary Fletcher, Searcy's pal at Eulenco, might know something. Marilyn has a date with him at noon."

"Thought you might get something out of Mrs. Searcy. She wouldn't talk to me." Burnbaum got up and headed for the door. "I'll keep in touch. If I hear anything, I'll let you know.... Say, Marilyn. A little advice: if you try another line of work, don't become a short order cook."

Marilyn scraped crumbs from Burnbaum's plate into the sink after the detective had left. "He was a big help."

"You can't blame him. It's up to us."

"I'm going to wash my hair now," Marilyn said.

"Why? It looks fine."

"For you, sure, but I've got a hot date at noon."

While Marilyn prepared for her rendezvous with Fletcher, McGraw drove to the Bottom Line Credit Bureau on East Sangamon Street in Springfield.

The credit bureau building was flanked by the Worldly Possessions pawn shop on the left and Norbert's Gun Shop on the right. When McGraw breezed into the credit bureau, a middle-aged woman with long black hair and the body of a fullback greeted him coolly. A sign on her desk identified her as "Carlie McLoon, Credit Coordinator".

"May I help you?" McLoon asked.

"I hope so," McGraw said. "I'm doing business with an out-of-state businessman, and we're talking big bucks. My whole life savings are in this deal. I want to make sure he's legit and he's not taking me to the cleaners, you know what I mean?"

"Of course."

"Well, I thought you could run a credit check on him."

"There's a thirty-five dollar fee," McLoon pointed out.

"That's fine."

"All right. What's his name?"

"Joseph Matlin Hersch. He lives in Mesa, Arizona."

"Spell the last name."

"H-e-r-s-c-h."

"Do you have the Social Security Number?"

"Yes, ma'am."

McGraw handed her a slip of paper bearing the number.

"First, we'll see if there's anything on the repository data bank. It will take a few minutes while I go online."

"I'll be back," McGraw said. "I'll just get a bite at the diner down the street."

"The food's lousy there."

"How's their credit rating?"

"It's lousy, too."

"You do enjoy your work, don't you?"

"It's not a job, it's a career!" McLoon declared.

"My thinking exactly, ma'am."

McGraw discovered the coffee and pastries at the Hungry Folks' Plantation Diner were as bad as McLoon had led him to believe. He was batting 0-for-2 on breakfasts. When McGraw returned to the Bottom Line Credit Bureau, he was noticeably weaker and paler.

"Ate at the Hungry Folks, didn't you?"

"Yes, ma'am."

"I warned you. … Here's the credit report, sport."

McGraw skimmed the computer printout detailing the credit history of Joseph Matlin Hersch. He was born August 12, 1956. Three previous addresses for Hersch in the Phoenix area were listed. Former employers included a telephone call center, a construction company and three talent agencies. He had trouble paying his credit card bills until about a year before.

After buying a large bottle of Maalox, McGraw returned to the Regal Court Apartments and showed Marilyn the credit report.

"Apparently he was a small-time actor recruited by the Jerome people for the role of a lifetime," McGraw said.

Marilyn noticed the clock. "Get ready, McGraw! I don't want to be late for my date with Fletcher!"

"I feel like a pimp," McGraw lamented. "Only I'm not getting any money out of it."

31

Pickup trucks and motorcycles packed the Tombstone Bar parking lot. Twangy country music performed by moonlighting middle-age wannabes drifted out from the bar.

McGraw preferred Chicago jazz over country music, but as he stood in the Tombstone Bar parking lot, dressed like a cowboy in a hat and jeans he picked up at K mart on his way back from Carlie McLoon's, he resolved to give country a try. Never let it be said Buck McGraw wouldn't do everything he could to get a story.

Marilyn sashayed to a table where Fletcher, decked out in plaid shirt and bluejeans, guzzled on a draw and flirted with a heavily rouged, extremely well-endowed woman wearing a "Divorced and Proud Of It!" tee shirt. When Fletcher realized Marilyn had actually showed up, he deserted the divorcee and escorted Marilyn to a table a few feet away.

"You didn't waste any time corralling another girl when

you thought I might not show up," Marilyn noted, a little hurt.

"As Robert Herrick wrote, 'Gather ye Rose-buds while ye may.' That was from his poem 'To the Virgins, to Make Much of Time'."

"So you're interested in poetry?" she asked.

"I majored in literature at Northwestern. That was after I majored in physics and before I majored in political science. I had a difficult time deciding what to do with my life. So, here I am, working at Eulenco and tearing down everything I believe in."

Marilyn asked the waitress for a Bud Lite.

"What is it you do at Eulenco?"

Fletcher took a swig of Coors. "Can't tell you, pretty lady. We've been warned not to say anything. I had to sign a confidentiality agreement saying I wouldn't discuss my work with outsiders."

"How important is your job?"

"I'm simply a cog in the machine. I'd hate to think I was responsible for getting that jerk Harry Jerome elected."

"Oh. So you really don't know what's going on."

That ruffled Fletcher's ego. "I wouldn't say that." He moved closer to her. "I know Murray Denton and his pals are pulling out all the stops to get Jerome elected, even blackmailing two Congressmen into supporting Harry and violating most campaign spending laws."

"Can you prove it?"

"Don't have anything in writing. Heard it from Morton Searcy and others. ... See, that's the kind of thing I can't talk about. It could be dangerous."

Marilyn laughed. "Dangerous? You work at a political consulting firm. What's dangerous about that?"

Fletcher gritted his teeth. "Look what they did to Searcy."

"What do you mean? Wasn't he killed in an airplane accident."

Fletcher leaned closer as he looked nervously around the bar. "That was no accident. These guys play rough."

Fletcher leaned to the side and peeked around a table that had blocked his view. "Say, isn't that your Chicago reporter friend over there—in the cowboy suit? What's the matter with him, anyway?"

Marilyn looked. McGraw was ogling a waitress' caboose as she left his table.

"That's him, the slimeball," Marilyn said.

"Don't think I like him. Something too smooth about him."

"Yes, well, he'll never have the down-to-earth charm of the locals."

"Obviously." Fletcher guzzled his beer.

"Did Morton ever say anything about Harry Jerome's real identity?"

"Don't know what you mean."

"He didn't say who he really was, or where he came from?"

"No. Far as I know, he's Harry Jerome from Ukiah, California."

"You said Morton's death was no accident."

Fletcher grimaced. "I've said too much already. Let's forget it."

"But he was your friend. What did he tell you? What did he find out about Eulenco? Maybe you can't do anything about it, but I can. Searcy's death was in vain if you haven't got the guts to do something about it! Sometimes, you've got to look deep inside yourself and find the courage to do what's right!"

Fletcher thought it over. Finally, he said, "Morton knew a lot of dirt about Eulenco. He said there was a conspiracy involving Jerome. I don't know any details. I didn't *want* to know any details. I didn't want to be involved, and I tried to get Morton to forget about it because worrying about it was making him a nervous wreck. But I do know one thing ... the day he was killed, he went to the state attorney general's office to spill the beans. ... Look what that got him."

"They couldn't protect him?"

"You're asking the wrong question. He didn't tell anyone but me he was going there, and he spoke to the state attorney general herself. So I don't think the question is *couldn't she protect him?*, but is *she in on the conspiracy, and is that the reason Morton was killed?*"

Fletcher noticed a stout man in a blue cardigan sweater had just walked in the door.

"I've got to get out of here," Fletcher said. "He's from Eulenco. I can't be seen talking to you."

"Farley Johnson. Research."

"Yes. One of Murray Denton's drinking buddies."

Johnson hadn't noticed them. Marilyn and Fletcher slipped on their jackets.

Just as Fletcher headed for the door, Johnson put down his beer and glanced around the bar. He spotted Fletcher, Marilyn and McGraw. For a moment, he seemed stunned. Then he reached for his cell phone.

As Fletcher left the bar. Marilyn hurried over to McGraw's table, where he was flirting with the waitress.

"Time to saddle up, McGraw. I think Farley Johnson spotted us."

"Yes, ma'am," McGraw said. He took a final draw on his

beer and plopped it on the table. He winked at the waitress. "Pardon me, young lady, while I go ridin' off into the sunset to help this poor defenseless creature."

"Come back, cowboy, and we'll see if you can hang on to a buckin' woman in bed," the waitress said.

"I will, or my name isn't Buck McGraw."

"I'm getting sick," Marilyn said. "After this is all over I'm going to have you put to sleep, like other dogs who outlived their usefulness."

"I like kinky," McGraw said, "but that sounds a little extreme."

Farley Johnson informed Murray Denton he spotted Fletcher in a bar with the reporters.

"Follow the reporters," Denton said. "When you find out where they're going, I'll send someone over to keep an eye on them."

Denton immediately called Roger Moss. "We'll need two of your men. And don't let them get trigger happy!"

"You still don't get it," Moss said. "The reporters have gotta be stopped *now!*"

"They were seen around Fletcher. He doesn't know much. Just keep an eye on the reporters so we'll know where they are if things heat up."

"Hell, Denton. How much hotter do you want things to get?"

Farley Johnson followed at a distance in his Pontiac as McGraw and Marilyn drove to Ann Pageant's apartment. Johnson called the location in to Denton. Ten minutes later, Wolfman showed up in his PT Cruiser.

"You can go," Wolfman grumbled. "I'll take over."

Wolfman was intimidating, but Farley wasn't sure he should leave. "I'd better check with Murray."

Wolfman got out of his pickup, reached into Farley's Pontiac, grabbed the cell phone and tossed it fifty feet into a clump of trees.

"Looks like your phone ain't workin', Johnson. Get the hell out of here!"

Farley's eyes opened wide. "Denton will hear about this! You can't go around tearing up Eulenco equipment!"

"I take my orders from Moss, not Denton," Wolfman growled.

Wolfman reached in and was about to drag Farley out of the Pontiac when Farley wrestled himself free and peeled down the street, leaving a trail of smoke. *"You're nuts!"* Farley bellowed.

Wolfman drove closer to the apartment complex and waited in the shadows. A few minutes later, Randall pulled up in his Cadillac and parked about forty feet away.

32

Detective Burnbaum had made himself comfortable in the apartment. He was sipping a soda and carving into a steak.

"You broke in?" McGraw asked.

"Had to. You didn't leave a key under the mat."

"I could have made you lunch," Marilyn said.

"You've got to be kidding. Give it up, honey. Some people can cook, some can't."

"You know, Burnbaum, nobody invited you here."

"I know, but you'd be lost without my help. So what did Fletcher tell you?"

"He said Searcy visited the state attorney general the day he died."

"No record of it," Burnbaum said.

"Fletcher thinks she may be in on the conspiracy," Marilyn said. "That would explain why there's no record."

Burnbaum shrugged. "Worth checking out, but you're running out of time. We'd better find out where the attorney general is today."

He pulled a cell phone out of his jacket. "Maggie? Burn-baum. ... Whoa. Hold on! That's not true. I don't call only when I need something. I've been busy. ... That's all right. I accept your apology. Now, what I need to know is where Kimball, the secretary of state, is today and where she'll be tonight. ... Maggie, put a cork in it. I'm probably all of those things, but I'm in a hurry. Just get the information."

Marilyn shook her head. "Did you miss the cops' seminar on people skills, Burnbaum?"

"I've got a job to do. Don't have time to grease the wheels. I leave that to politicians."

Burnbaum pulled back the curtain at a living room window and sized up the neighborhood.

"You're coming up in the world. You got *two* men following you."

"Well, that was always my dream," Marilyn noted.

Burnbaum's cell phone rang.

"Yeah. ... Okay. Thanks, Maggie. I owe you one. ... All right, I owe you a dozen." He turned to the reporters. "Kimball is in Chicago. She'll be home in Springfield this evening. Probably about seven."

"All right! Marilyn and I will be there."

"Those two goons out front will try to follow you," Burnbaum said. "Be careful."

33

Across town, Murray Denton studied Eulenco's final polls. It appeared Jerome's surge in the final days would be enough for a victory.

Denton popped the lid on a Coors, nibbled on a piece of pizza and watched a few minutes of a television movie about a mother dying of cancer. Her spouse had just revealed he was having an affair with a heart attack victim when Reverend Drury dropped by Denton's office.

Drury pulled up a chair. "What are you doing, Denton? Watching teevee as the campaign collapses around you?"

Denton flipped off the television. The cancer victim and cheating hubby would need to work things out without him. "Everything's under control. Nothing's collapsing."

"Have you found the reporters?"

"Moss has two men birddogging them. Quit worrying. The reporters have zilch. They can't print anything because they can't prove anything. Harry's response to the allegations about Harry's death was brilliant."

"Stop deluding yourself. The truth is we don't know what they have. We can't just wait around. If this ship springs one more leak, the whole thing could sink. You've got to deal with the problem!"

"Moss sent you over to 'reason' with me, didn't he?"

"It wasn't just Moss. We are *all* concerned you aren't dealing with the problem."

Denton nodded toward the pizza. "Help yourself."

Drury reached for a slice and a napkin.

"What did you preach on Sunday morning, Drury? Love and compassion? Or what to do with the body after you kill someone?"

"You don't like me much, do you, Denton?"

"We are involved in a business undertaking. Liking you or disliking you doesn't enter into it. … But since you ask … No, I don't like you, Drury. And I don't respect you. You're one of those people who wants to run everyone else's lives. You want people to be like you. … I can't imagine why."

"You're not fit to judge me, Denton. Talk about running people's lives—you're a political consultant! You cajole people, manipulate them, confuse them, deceive them to get what you want."

"You're right. And I'm good at my job. Hell, I could take a Nazi, wrap him in the American flag and voters would flock to the polls to elect him. Before you know it, he'd be watering down our freedoms until they're meaningless. … You're right, Drury. We both manipulate people. The difference is I hate myself for it. You're proud of it."

"I feel sorry for you, Denton. You're a lost soul. You don't have a strong belief in God to sustain you, so you turn to liquor."

Denton slammed the beer can on the table. "God? What do you know of God, you self-righteous hypocrite? Your god is one you created in your own image … one who tolerates bigotry and lies and greed. From what I've heard, the real God isn't like that. God doesn't stir up hatred. He doesn't despise the starving. And He doesn't condone murder!"

Drury was unmoved. "You're the expert on murder, I believe."

Denton sighed. "All I did was tell Moss to take care of the Searcy problem. Next thing I know, he's killed nineteen people and I'm in this deeper than I ever thought possible."

"All the more reason to get rid of the reporters. They're the only thing standing between us and the Governor's Mansion. You already racked up nineteen deaths. Two more won't make much difference."

Denton fished another piece of pizza out of the box. "Look, I'm on top of the situation. If they jeopardize the project, they'll be eliminated."

Drury wiped the crumbs off his mouth and rose out of his chair. "Just don't wait too long."

"For a preacher, you're awfully damn bloodthirsty."

"For a political consultant, you're awfully squeamish."

"Get out of here, Drury. Go find some orphans to torment."

34

A cold, strong breeze swept down over Chicago and its sub-
urbs that afternoon. Towering buildings in the Loop acted
as a wind tunnel, intensifying the bone-chilling blasts of
air. Rick Slater hurried from the parking lot to the *Chronicle*
building bundled in a heavy overcoat. To Slater, the howl-
ing winds were an omen. He was in for a long, harrowing
day.

"Afternoon, Mr. Slater," the security man called out as
the state editor barged into the lobby. "Cold enough for
you?"

Slater grunted a greeting. Was it cold enough for him?
No, he'd prefer to see it thirty, forty degrees colder. Of course
it was cold enough for him! Why did people say things like
that to him? To drive him nuts?

As he stepped into the elevator, he tried to catch his
breath. He must calm down. He knew it was McGraw that
made him irritable. It was McGraw that was making his life
miserable. He shouldn't take it out on others. So much was

riding on this day, so much depended on McGraw ... Oh, Lord. The *Chronicle* was in big trouble.

Throughout the building, the next day's election-morning edition of the *Chronicle* already was taking shape. Deadlines for feature pages passed; those pages were given final approval. Display ads from Macy's, Carson Pirie Scott and several dozen other stores had been proofed and OK'd and were ready to go. In the composing room, eight pages of classified ads were laid out on computer terminals using page composition software. In the pressroom, crews cleaned the massive presses. Editors of the Internet version of the *Chronicle* updated the web site as news flowed in.

Slater checked his e-mail and discovered McGraw had forwarded the front pages from Germany. Then he called two downstate correspondents and edited copy for pages with early deadlines. He was deep in thought when George Purnell ambled up to his desk.

"What do you hear from McGraw?" the managing editor asked. "Does he have the story?"

"I'm sure he's wrapping it up. We'll get it, George."

"I hope so. Our lawyers are upstairs with the publisher, ready to check the story for legal problems."

"He e-mailed me copies of the front pages of German newspapers reporting Harry Jerome's death. I e-mailed them to you. We need to translate the stories into English."

"No problem."

"What time does the bash for Harry start at the Ritz Carlton?" Slater asked.

"Eight. We'll have five reporters and three photographers over there."

Slater nodded. "Harry's big moment in the spotlight and we're going to turn out the lights."

"If we're wrong, they'll be turning out the lights on the *Chronicle*!"

"McGraw will check out everything thoroughly."

"You really are gullible, Slater. When this is all over, I've got a tract of land thirty-five feet under Lake Michigan I'll sell you."

As Purnell trotted back to his office, Slater reached for a bottle of Pepto Bismol he kept in a desk drawer. Then he called McGraw.

"Did you call me a 'very demented person' when I phoned you this morning?"

"I don't remember. Sounds like something I'd say."

"I got the files you sent—the photos of the German newspaper pages—and the stories are being translated. Did you notice the note that came with the files? From someone named Hans ..."

"I didn't see any note."

Slater turned to his computer. "It says: 'Murderer caught. Vacation over. Faxed you copies of Jerome story. Send us your story. Please enclose photo of your girlfriend—topless.' What's that about?"

"Hans has been helpful, but he's a little sleazy. I'll send him a photo of your wife—naked. It'll appear in their national edition."

"Not unless they're hell-bent on losing circulation ... Look, McGraw, I need the Jerome story by nine tonight or we'll miss the downstate edition. Have you got it?"

"We have a few details to nail down."

Slater lowered his voice. "But you've got all the dope about the campaign and who's behind it. Right?"

"Well, Slater, the truth is ... we hope to get that tonight."

Now Slater was yelling. *"What? What the hell are you wait-*

ing for? We need the story, McGraw! You're not at the Exposer, *you're in the big leagues. Bullshit doesn't cut it. Results do!"*

"I'll have it, Slater! Stop worrying. Have I ever let you down?"

Slater hung up. "We're dead," he mumbled.

35

Moss ordered both Randall and Wolfman to stake out the Regal Court Apartments because Denton didn't want to take a chance on losing track of the two reporters.

At five that evening, McGraw and Marilyn left Ann Pageant's apartment and drove off in the *Chronicle*'s Buick.

Randall, trailing them in his Cadillac, reported in to Moss: "We're rolling, Delphi."

"Me, too," chimed in Wolfman, who brought up the rear in his PT Cruiser. "Tell me again who I rub out—the reporters or Randall."

"No one," Moss radioed back. "Least not yet."

"Why is that slimeball on this job?" Randall asked Delphi.

"You mean Wolfman?"

"Yeah."

"I needed two bodies, 'case they split up."

"If Wolfman keeps it up, he'll be the first to go," warned Randall.

McGraw eyeballed the rear view mirror. He noticed the Cadillac. "We're being followed," he told Marilyn. "Let's lose him."

He floored the accelerator. The Buick roared off, quickly hitting seventy in a thirty-five zone.

Randall stayed close behind. Wolfman was a half block behind Randall.

McGraw wove through traffic, took two hard rights, then stopped in a bank's parking lot.

"Speed on by 'em, Randall," Wolfman said. "They'll think they lost you. I'll watch 'em."

"Just don't lose 'em," Randall warned.

"Lose 'em? You know who you're talkin' to?" Wolfman growled.

"Yeah. A psycho with a superiority complex. A dangerous combination."

Randall's Cadillac roared on past the bank. Wolfman pulled up a half block from the bank and kept an eye on the Buick.

McGraw was satisfied they had lost the tail and didn't notice the PT Cruiser. He drove on.

Darkness had settled over the city by the time the reporters pulled up a hundred feet away from the entrance to a rambling two-story ranch-style house. McGraw and Marilyn waited in the Buick.

Wolfman called Moss. "Candlelight Drive. Sign in front of the house says Kettle Hill."

"Kettle Hill?" Moss repeated. "That's Attorney General Kimball's home! We got trouble."

"Now can I whack 'em?" asked Wolfman.

"Not yet!"

Randall heard Wolfman call in the location. Five minutes later he pulled up behind Wolfman.

As the reporters and Denton's tough guys waited for Kimball to show up, Moss called Denton.

"The reporters are sittin' outside Kettle Hill."

"If they talk to Kimball," Denton said, "and it looks like she's cooperating, we'll have no choice."

"You mean knock 'em off."

"As a last resort."

"That'll make Wolfman's day," Moss noted.

McGraw and Marilyn listened to mellow rock on the car radio as they waited. At one point, Marilyn used her cell phone to make a call. "Twenty eight thirteen Candlelight Drive," she said. And hung up.

"I gave Runyon the location," she told McGraw. "Sort of an insurance policy, so Channel 10 will know where I am in case I'm attacked by Denton's people ... or a half-crazed reporter from Chicago."

"Three hours till deadline and we haven't got the story!" McGraw lamented. "Jerome will be governor and we'll be at the *National Exposer* writing about three-headed pigs with sexual hangups."

"I've dated a few."

Twenty minutes later a pizza delivery van pulled up beside the Buick.

"Pepperoni and sausage pizza?" the delivery boy asked.

"No!" McGraw growled. "Get outta here!"

"I ordered it," Marilyn said. "Pay the kid, McGraw."

"You ordered a pizza?" McGraw gasped in disbelief. *"You don't have pizzas delivered when you're on a stakeout!"*

"You do if you're hungry."

McGraw pounded the steering wheel. Then he decided he might as well accept what was happening.

"Got any cola?" he asked.

"Sure," said the kid.

"Two-liter bottle. It's going to be a long night." He turned to Marilyn. "You want a drink?"

"Root beer," she said.

The kid totalled it up. "Sixteen dollars and eighty five cents."

McGraw gave the kid a twenty. "Now get out of here! You're interfering with an investigation."

The kid hopped back into his van. "What are you investigating? How long it takes to deliver pizza?"

"Smart alec kid," McGraw mumbled. He turned to Marilyn. "Don't ever do that again!"

He chomped into his pizza. It wasn't bad. "And if you do it again, get me the deluxe, with all the trimmings. ... You didn't call Runyon. You called the pizza restaurant!"

Marilyn shrugged. "I told them earlier what I wanted and said I'd call in the location this evening."

McGraw rolled down the car windows about an inch to air out the Buick. He didn't want it smelling like pizza when he returned it to the *Chronicle*.

After they finished off a couple slices of pizza, Marilyn skimmed through information about the Illinois attorney general's office she had downloaded off the Internet that afternoon.

"McGraw, do you know the name of the attorney general?"

"Of course. Betsy Kimball."

"Betsy *French* Kimball. Do you remember the name of that woman on the Committee to Elect Jerome—the one we couldn't find?"

"Betsy French. You don't think—"

"Why not? There's been a lot of press about bad blood between Dodge and Kimball because she favored giving Martin Hudson the loan guarantees he wanted."

"Someone from Dodge's administration is on the Committee to Elect Jerome? That's a real stretch."

"It would explain why there's no record of Searcy spilling his guts to the attorney general's office."

"We've got no proof," McGraw pointed out.

"She doesn't know that. Maybe we can bluff her into confessing."

"It's all we've got," McGraw conceded. "But if you're wrong—she's the attorney general. She could lock us up and throw away the key!"

A knock on the car window next to Marilyn startled the reporters. It was Burnbaum.

"You got balls, Marilyn," he said. "McGraw, you should wear a dress."

"Don't be a smartass, Burnbaum. I didn't say I wouldn't confront Kimball. I was saying it could land us in a lot of trouble."

"I'm with Marilyn. Go for it. ... By the way, did you know two cars are following you? One more, you need a parade permit ... I'd say those dudes know what you're doing here. They'll probably try to get rid of you. ... Hey, pizza! Can I have a slice?"

"Help yourself."

Burnbaum climbed in the back seat and grabbed a piece of pizza.

A few minutes after seven, a white Mercedes pulled into the drive in front of the house.

"There she is!" Burnbaum said.

Kimball opened her front door and went inside.

"This is it," McGraw told Marilyn. "If we don't wrap up the story in two hours, Harry will be governor and we'll be unemployed."

"Or possibly dead," Burnbaum suggested.

36

The clock in the *Chicago Chronicle* newsroom advanced inexorably, oblivious to the anguish it was causing. It was already 7:15 P.M., and Rick Slater had an unsettling feeling Purnell was right. They were in deep trouble.

On a television set a few feet from the State Desk could be seen the raucous crowd at Harry's election-eve bash. The announcer described the scene at the Ritz Carlton:

"Several thousand people are here, waiting for Harry Jerome to speak. To them, it seems a foregone conclusion that Jerome will be the next governor of Illinois. Indeed, this affair seems more like a coronation than a campaign rally."

Purnell approached the State Desk looking like an expectant father whose wife was three hours overdue. He pulled up a chair and squatted on it.

"I don't suppose we have the story," he said.

"Not yet," Slater admitted.

"Right. That would be asking too much. After all, we've got another hour and a forty minutes till deadline."

On the television screen, a Jerome supporter bashed a cameraman in the head with her purse.

"I'll have another front page ready to go in case we don't get the story," Purnell said. "We can't risk everything on McGraw. ... Have you read supermarket tabloids like the *Exposer*? They're beyond weird. Must be something they put in the air conditioning in Florida. Makes people crazy. They lose touch with reality."

"Sometimes reality gets pretty weird, too," Slater noted.

"I bet McGraw is holed up in a hotel room, sweatin' like a gorilla in heat because he promised us a wild story he can't deliver."

"Don't think so, George. There are a lot of unexplained things about Jerome and his campaign."

Purnell got up and put the chair back where he found it. "Let's hope they're not unexplained come tomorrow morning. ... You know, I've always believed in thinking outside the box. Why should criminal enterprises be the only ones to use hit men? Legitimate businesses like the *Chronicle* could order hits on people instead of firing them. Save a lot on pension and health care costs."

"George ..."

"Yeah?"

"That's not thinking outside the box. That's thinking outside the law. Your drinking is frying your brain."

"Maybe. But this isn't the night to stop."

37

Burnbaum said he would keep an eye on Eulenco's men while McGraw and Marilyn confronted Kimball. The reporters made their way to Kimball's front porch, where Marilyn knocked on the door.

A half minute passed before Betsy Kimball opened the door. She had swapped her business suit for a maroon pullover sweater and black cotton twill slacks. A cigarette dangled from her right hand.

The reporters introduced themselves. Kimball showed them into the expansive living room, where a glistening glass chandelier hung from the ceiling. The plush white carpet was an inch and a half thick. The black leather sofa could hold the Chicago Symphony, with room left over for the brass section of the Boston Pops. On a big screen television, the crowd at Jerome's Chicago rally applauded loudly as Farrell Foundation President Richard Dunnington enumerated the candidate's virtues:

"Harry Jerome is uniquely qualified to run this state! In times like this, when people distrust politicians and their motives, it's

good to know there's someone like Harry Jerome around — a candidate whose integrity, compassion and experience set him head and shoulders above everyone else."

"Makes you feel warm all over," McGraw suggested.

Kimball muted the volume on the television.

"What can I do for you?" the attorney general said.

"Should we call you Betsy Kimball? Or Betsy French?" asked Marilyn.

"French was my maiden name. When I divorced Bruce Kimball, I didn't bother to change my name because voters know me as Betsy Kimball."

"And you are the Betsy French who is a member of the Committee to Elect Harry Jerome?" McGraw asked.

She seemed stunned by the question. "No! That's the craziest thing I've ever heard."

"Might as well admit it," McGraw said. "We know all about Harry Jerome's corrupt campaign and your involvement in it. The story will be plastered all over front pages and television screens tomorrow morning. We've got the whole ball of wax ... Harry Jerome's death sixteen years ago, an imposter running as Jerome, the phony holdup in Chicago that made Jerome a hero, your role in the death of Morton Searcy, your position on the committee to elect ..."

"We know it's a conspiracy to take over the state government," Marilyn said. "We know *you* are involved. This is your last chance to tell your side of it before the whole thing explodes in your face!"

The visitors waited anxiously. Would Kimball go for the bait? Euphoric scenes from Jerome's rally in Chicago filled the television screen, contradicting the picture McGraw was painting of doom and disaster.

Kimball took a long draw from the cigarette. "It is a

mess, isn't it? ... It's true, I'm on the committee to elect Jerome."

"Why didn't you openly admit you supported Jerome?"

"Harry's people said I could be more effective by letting people believe I supported the governor. I was able to give Jerome's people information that helped them."

"What happened when Morton Searcy showed up at your office, saying he wanted to blow the lid off Jerome's campaign?"

"I called Murray Denton and told him Searcy came to see me. That's all. Next day, I read about the plane crash that killed Searcy and eighteen others. I couldn't believe it! I had nothing to do with that."

After a long pause, Kimball said, in a low, shaky voice. "I told them they couldn't get away with it. I told them that all along."

"Who did you tell?" McGraw asked, trying to conceal his excitement. "George Madden is behind it, right?"

"Madden?" She laughed. "Do you really think George Madden has the brains or the clout for something like this?"

"Then who?" Marilyn asked.

Kimball paused. "Martin Hudson."

"*What?*" Marilyn and McGraw said in unison.

"That's right. Hudson is desperate to build that huge global entertainment and communication network—his corporation's future depends on it—but he can't handle the financing. And he'd never get it from the state with Dodge in the governor's office."

"So his only hope is to elect a governor who will give him the backing he needs!" Marilyn declared.

"Correct."

"Who else is involved?" McGraw asked.

"George Madden. Murray Denton. George Hersch ..." Kimball sighed. She decided she might as well name the others. "Pastor Drury. Richard Dunnington. Sue Ellen Jerrell. And that kid ..."

"What kid?" asked McGraw.

"That Chicago reporter. I think his name was Carl something."

"Yorbly?"

"That's right."

McGraw was stunned. Yorbly was the *Chronicle* reporter he had replaced on the Jerome story, the one who sent Slater nothing but PR dribble. Clearly, the conspirators had all the bases covered. McGraw wouldn't have been assigned to the Jerome campaign if Yorbly hadn't had back surgery.

"Jerome's running mate, Karl Olson—he wasn't part of the conspiracy?" Marilyn asked.

"No."

A shot of Harry sitting on the platform filled the television screen.

"All right," McGraw said. "We know why Hudson did it. Why did the others join the conspiracy?"

"We all stood to make a fortune if Hudson's project was built. He promised us a chunk of the profits. But I don't think that preacher, Drury, did it just for the money. He wanted someone like Jerome in the governor's office, someone he could use as a mouthpiece for his views."

Randall and Wolfman snuck up to Kimball's house and peered in a living room window. Kimball seemed to be shaken. And talking a lot.

The freelance tough guys backed off a few feet. Randall called Moss on his cell phone.

"Looks like Kimball's spilling her guts," Randall said. "We'd better stop her now!"

"Okay. Do it! Make it look like Kimball died in a break-in gone bad. Take the reporters' bodies out to the Lincoln Tomb. There's a secret room. The bodies won't be found for years."

"How did they pick Hersch to be the candidate?" Marilyn asked Kimball.

"Denton contacted employment agencies in dozens of large cities telling them he needed an actor for a commercial he was filming. When he had several possibilities, he investigated them and narrowed the list. Hersch looked the part."

Suddenly the lights and the television shut off, leaving the house in darkness.

"Denton's henchmen cut off the power!" McGraw said.

"You were followed here?" Kimball asked. For the first time, she was frightened.

"Afraid so," Marilyn said. "We've got to leave."

"Take me with you!" Kimball insisted. "You can't leave me here. They'll kill me!"

Kimball led the way to the back door. On the way out, she grabbed a pile of printouts, memos and documents.

Wolfman burst into the house and searched for the targets. Randall waited behind a bush in the backyard and opened fire when McGraw, Marilyn and Kimball appeared at the back door. Burnbaum fired three shots. Randall dropped. He hadn't seen it coming.

McGraw, Marilyn and Kimball dashed for Kimball's Mercedes, parked about fifteen feet away. They piled in, McGraw in the driver's seat, Kimball next to him, Marilyn in back. A few seconds later, Burnbaum jumped into the back seat.

"Haul ass!" Burnbaum hollered.

McGraw hit the accelerator as Wolfman ran out of the house, firing at them. The Mercedes roared down Candle-light Drive.

Randall, wounded, limped to his Cadillac. Wolfman ran to the Cadillac, jumped in the passenger side and grabbed Randall's shotgun. As Randall drove, Wolfman fired at the Mercedes.

In the Mercedes, Kimball nodded toward the back seat. "I take it you know him."

"Right," McGraw said. "Burnbaum's a Chicago cop."

"Pleased to meet ya," Burnbaum said. "You're under arrest."

"You're out of your jurisdiction," Kimball pointed out.

"Maybe so," Burnbaum said. "You're still under arrest."

In the Cadillac, Randall dripped blood on the seat. Wolfman radioed Moss asking for reinforcements.

38

Marilyn nodded toward the stack of papers Kimball had grabbed. "Is that the proof there's a conspiracy?"

"No, my utility bills," Kimball said sarcastically. "Of course I brought proof. I know how the system works. If I cooperate, I'll get a lighter sentence."

Randall fought to stay conscious and control the Cadillac as Wolfman fired the shotgun at the Mercedes. So far, he had knocked out a tail light on the Mercedes and crippled two pedestrians.

McGraw pressed the Mercedes' accelerator to the floor.

"I felt safer working for the other side," Kimball lamented.

Brakes squealed as McGraw wheeled around a corner at high speed and weaved through traffic on Chatham Road. Kimball switched on the car radio. In Chicago, Sue Ellen Jerrell was praising Jerome.

"I usually tell people they can take control of their lives and acquire wealth beyond their wildest dreams. Well, tonight I'm telling you that you can control your future by voting tomorrow for Harry Jerome!"

A bullet hit the rear of the Mercedes. Kimball lowered the volume on the radio.

"Head for Channel 10!" Marilyn said. "I can get my story on the air and you can e-mail yours to Chicago."

McGraw gritted his teeth. "You wouldn't be trying to steal my scoop, would you?"

A bullet shattered their rear window. The Cadillac was close behind.

"Sometimes I think you're from another planet," Marilyn shrieked. "You work for a morning paper that takes seven hours to get from the presses to readers. Channel 10 can air the news in seconds. It's not my fault you're living in the past. *I'm putting the story on the air tonight!*"

McGraw pounded the steering wheel. "I can't believe you're trying to steal my story! I thought we shared everything fifty-fifty. I ought to stop and let that greaseball have you!"

"Oh, Lord," moaned the attorney general. "Maybe I'll get out at the corner up there."

"Not a chance," Burnbaum said.

"I don't think I like you," Kimball told him.

"I hear that a lot."

McGraw swerved down an alley. When the alley dumped out onto Monroe Street, he narrowly avoided hitting a truck. He swerved onto the street and immediately turned into a parking lot. They ducked their heads as the Cadillac sped by.

McGraw tried to reason with Marilyn. "Just sit on the story till tomorrow morning."

"Would you sit on it for ten hours?" she asks. "This is a game-changing story, and it's all ours!"

"I could drive straight to Chicago so you couldn't air it tonight," McGraw said, thinking out loud.

"Use your brain, McGraw. If you drive up there, you'd miss *your* deadline and it would be thirty-two hours from now before people would see the story. By then, Harry would be the governor-elect. Any way you look at it, you lose!"

McGraw sighed as he started up the Mercedes. "Not if I tie you up and throw you in the trunk for forty-eight hours."

"Get serious, McGraw. It's not my fault you work on deadlines out of the Stone Age. Let's get over to my station before Denton's goons find us!"

McGraw headed toward the TV station, but a block down the street Wolfman spotted them and the Cadillac hauled off in pursuit, shotgun blazing. A bullet passed within an inch of Marilyn's head.

Wolfman radioed the location in to Moss.

Two minutes later, a Dodge Charger and a Kia shot out of a side street. Inside the Charger were George Madden and Murray Denton. Madden hit the brakes and blocked the path of the Mercedes. Eulenco security men in the Kia pulled up beside the Charger.

McGraw slammed on his brakes, screeched into a 270-degree turn and roared down a side street. He ran another red light and narrowly missed a power pole.

Kimball turned the sound on the radio up for a minute. At the rally, Rev. Drury introduced Jerome:

"This election is the high point of Harry Jerome's lifelong quest to serve his fellow Americans. He never imagined when he

was a boy living in a small California town that one day he would be running for governor of the great state of Illinois. It is a dream come true!"

"If I don't get the story first, Slater will kill me," McGraw moaned. "I tell you what, Marilyn—the *Chronicle* will hire you. Fifteen grand a year more than you're making at your piddling TV station!"

"Make it thirty," Marilyn said, "and I want to hear Slater okay it."

"Deal," McGraw replied.

McGraw hung a left at high speed, but the gunmen stayed with him.

"Why did they give their candidate Harry Jerome's name and background?" Marilyn asked the attorney general. "They must have known someone might snoop around, looking into his past."

"That's the kicker," Kimball said. "Denton said nobody but Morton Searcy knew Harry Jerome had really existed. Searcy was in charge of coming up with a name and background for the candidate. Searcy was lazy, so he used the background of a real person. He and Harry Jerome had been roommates at San Jose State."

Bullets chewed up the trunk of the Mercedes as it raced toward Channel 10's studios. Two police cars joined in the chase, behind the Cadillac, the Kia and the Charger.

On the radio, Jerome worked the crowd into a fever pitch.

"Together, there is nothing we can't do! Turn your back on the governor's empty promises and shallow liberalism. As governor, I will work to create a better life for everyone in this wonderful state!"

Roger Moss pushed the Charger to its limits as Murray Denton's blood pressure escalated by the minute. Everything depended on stopping the reporters and the attorney general before they could tell their story to the police—or get it to the public. "Hold on!" Moss growled, as his Charger bolted through another red light.

"I don't think we need to worry about going to jail," Denton grumbled. "We won't survive this ride. Slow down!"

Moss squeezed the accelerator even harder. "Like hell! It's time to separate the men from the boys!"

Moss' cell phone rang. Denton picked it up. A voice from the Cadillac crackled, "Everything's under control. We've got 'em right where we want 'em!"

Denton shook his head. "How do you figure that, Wolfman? They're seventy feet in front of you!"

"If they were seventy feet behind us, we'd lose 'em for sure."

Denton hung up. "Part of the problem is that you hire idiots."

"Quit complaining and make yourself useful," Moss said. "There's a shotgun on the back seat."

"Like I know how to use it ..."

"You'd better learn real quick."

Denton grabbed the shotgun, fired and hit the windshield—of the Cadillac with Wolfman and Randall inside.

"Now try hitting the Mercedes," Moss said.

The phone rang. "Who the hell is shooting at us?" Wolfman demanded.

"No speaka the English," Denton said.

39

The Mercedes screeched into Channel 10's parking lot. Marilyn, McGraw and Kimball dashed into the building. Burnbaum crouched behind the Mercedes and fired at Eulenco's three cars as they rolled into the lot.

Matt Lorry, the Channel 10 security guard, stuck his head out the main entrance. "What the hell is going on?"

"Harry Jerome's people are trying to kill us," Marilyn said. "The cop behind the Mercedes is on our side."

Lorry fired away at men crouching behind the Eulenco cars. They returned fire. Bullets whizzed past the guard's head.

"Holy mackerel," Lorry said. The police cars pulled in and blocked Eulenco's cars. A bullet struck Moss in the shoulder. Wolfman got it in the leg. Denton put his hands up. Burnbaum and the police took charge as Lorry disarmed Randall, who was already bleeding.

McGraw, Marilyn and the attorney general hustled to the newsroom, where television monitors were tuned to Jerome's rally. Jerome was still talking ...

"This is the culmination of all that we have been working for! Tomorrow, by casting your vote for me, you will set this state on a new path to prosperity and law-and-order. This will be our finest hour!"

"Enjoy your hour," McGraw said. He peeked out a window to see how the skirmish between Jerome's people and the cops was going. The cops had it under control.

Marilyn told Jed Runyon about the latest developments as McGraw called Slater.

"Let me talk to the Terror of the State Desk."

Slater came on the line a few seconds later.

"You got it?"

"We've got it! Seven conspirators hired Joseph Hersch to pose as Harry Jerome so they could win the election, run the government and make a lot of money. I've got the names, and Attorney General Kimball is telling all—she was in on it. And you'll love this ... the big cheese behind it all is *Martin Hudson!"*

"My Lord! Are you sure!"

"No, we're pulling names out of a hat ... *Of course I'm sure!* There's bad news, too—Carl Yorbly was part of the conspiracy."

"Holy cow! ... All right, McGraw. Get the story to me fast. I need it in an hour for the downstate edition!"

"One more thing, Slater. To keep the story our property, I told Marilyn we'd hire her at fifty grand a year. Will you confirm that?"

"Is she worth it, McGraw?"

McGraw hesitated and looked at Marilyn. "Yeah, she's worth it."

"All right."

Marilyn took the phone.

"Agreed," Slater said. "Fifty grand a year."

Lorry staggered into the newsroom, muttered he was getting too old for security work, and collapsed into a chair.

McGraw pushed Lorry out of the chair—the desk in front of it was the only one not being used—and hurriedly began typing the story on his laptop. A few minutes later he became vaguely aware Marilyn was talking about the story on one of the television sets scattered throughout the newsroom. She was reporting the story on Channel 10 News!

"... a result of a joint investigation by Channel 10 and the Chicago Chronicle. *The mastermind behind the conspiracy was Martin Hudson, the millionaire Chicago media tycoon."*

McGraw felt sick. The story obviously meant more to Marilyn than McGraw did. So after all they had been through together, this was how their relationship would end.

With the deadline fast approaching, McGraw continued typing, but as soon as Marilyn was off-camera he confronted her.

"You reneged on our deal!" McGraw roared.

"What deal? You asked me if I wanted to work for the *Chronicle* for fifty thousand a year. I said yes. I said nothing about keeping the story off the air. I worked this story on Channel 10's time, McGraw! I owe it to them! Besides, you will still be first with the full story in the *Chronicle*—the complete details. You can still win your Pulitzer."

McGraw slammed a fist against a wall and returned to his computer. He resumed typing. "You are the craziest broad I've ever met. I should have thrown you off the plane when you pretended to be my nurse. Nobody would have blamed me!"

"But McGraw," Marilyn said, "my big salary will come in handy when we're living together in Chicago."

McGraw calmed down and looked at her. "You're not leaving me?"

"Just try to get rid of me."

She was right about that. He had tried before. If Marilyn didn't want to leave it was nearly impossible to get rid of her. Maybe he had found a woman who would stay with him after all. Wait till Morelli and Reardon heard about that!

Marilyn planted a moist kiss on McGraw's lips. The tough guy melted a little.

"Save it for later," he grunted. "I've got a story to finish. Besides, nobody's going to see the story on your piddling little station. They'll read about it in the *Chronicle*."

40

As George Purnell tinkered with a page layout in the *Chicago Chronicle* newsroom, Rick Slater hustled up to his desk.

"You mean the front page isn't finished?" Slater thundered. "I thought you'd have it ready to go!"

"Who would have thought McGraw would really get the story?" Purnell mumbled.

"Jeez, George," Slater whined, loud enough for the city staff to hear, "you ought to have more confidence in our reporters."

"I do. It's *National Exposer* people I don't have faith in. But it looks like McGraw came through. That's all the crow I'm going to eat. Get out of here. I'm busy."

"Sure thing, George. ... Uh, I think I'd boost the size of the headline a little, and make that photo of Jerome and Martin Hudson a three column."

"Get out of here!"

41

Martin Hudson and his wife Jenine arrived at the Ritz Carlton ballroom as Jerome was ending his speech. Jerome had presented his arguments and now was asking for a commitment from voters:

"When you go to the polls tomorrow, you will be presented with a unique opportunity — an opportunity to change the course of government in our state forever. By casting a vote for me, you will reject the tired, corrupt politics of the past and create a glorious future for you, your family and the entire state of Illinois!"

Supporters rose to their feet and cheered wildly. Jerome smiled broadly and shook hands with everyone within reach.

Hudson left his wife in the company of one of his vice presidents and began working his way through the crowd. When he was forty feet from the podium, Jamieson came over and greeted him. The noise was deafening, so Jamieson nodded toward one of the exits. He led the way as Hudson followed.

In the hallway, the cheering was less overbearing.

"They're eating it up!" Jamieson said. "This should clinch it!"

Hudson relaxed. "I hope you're right. I bet the farm on Harry. You took care of the two reporters who were snooping around?"

"Denton said they wouldn't bother us again."

"Why did he cut it so close to the wire?"

"Who knows?"

"Jerome looks weary. Is he going to be all right?"

"Should be fine," Jamieson said. "It's been a long campaign. He's exhausted. We all are."

"It will be over tomorrow," Hudson noted. "And when he takes office, my problems will be over."

Suddenly the cheering of the crowd stopped.

"What's going on?" Hudson asked.

"I don't know," Jamieson said.

They quickly walked back inside. On the large screen appeared a news announcer.

"At this point, details are sketchy. What we know for sure is that press associations are reporting that the Chicago Chronicle *and Springfield's Channel 10 say Harry Jerome and his entire campaign have been a fraud ... that the real Harry Jerome is dead and the candidate is Joseph Hersch, an Arizonan whom conspirators selected to campaign for the governor's office. Their primary goal, according to the news reports, was to give loan guarantees and millions of dollars in state funds to the billion-dollar Hudson Entertainment and Communications Complex proposed by Chicago media mogul Martin Hudson. Many of the conspirators have been arrested in Springfield. The arrests of Joseph Hersch, Martin Hudson, Press Secretary Duncan Jamieson and other advisors is imminent in Chicago, where the candidate is holding a gigantic election-eve rally."*

As the newscast ended, policemen entered the ballroom and rounded up the conspirators.

42

An hour and a half later, the last plates were locked on massive presses in the basement of the *Chicago Chronicle* building and the downstate edition rolled off the presses. The noise was deafening.

Slater fished a copy off a conveyer belt and handed it to Purnell. They scanned the front page banner headline:

Chicago Chronicle
HARRY JEROME A FRAUD!
CONSPIRATORS TRIED TO PLACE 'PUPPET' IN STATE'S TOP OFFICE

"McGraw came through for us," Slater said.

"Yep," Purnell said. "Don't know which is more startling. The Jerome conspiracy, or McGraw getting the story."

"Admit it, Purnell. McGraw did a helluva job. Old man Bellingham would have been proud of his paper tonight."

"I reckon you're right, Slater." Purnell rolled the paper up and stuck it in his coat pocket. "Well, this is quite an occasion. See you tomorrow. I'm going to get drunk."

VIII

Election Day

43

The next morning, McGraw, Marilyn and Fletcher looked on as Murray Denton was booked at Springfield police headquarters, along with George Madden, Pastor Lawrence Drury, Richard Dunnington, Betsy French Kimball, Roger Moss and Eulenco's security force. In Chicago, Martin Hudson, Joseph Hersch, Sue Ellen Jerrell and Carl Yorbly made their first appearances before a judge.

McGraw snatched a copy of the *Chicago Chronicle* from a vending machine and showed Marilyn the headline plastered across the front page.

"It's more impressive when you see it in print," McGraw suggested.

"Not really."

Slater called McGraw.

"Harry Jerome Junior and his family were found

unharmed in a basement in Ukiah. The man who was paid to guard them was arrested. By the way, I e-mailed your story to your pal Hans in Germany. He called back to say they ran it on page three, sandwiched between nude art of a hooker and a yarn about the Loch Ness monster swallowing a Toyota. I think Hans and that newspaper deserve each other."

George Madden received a phone call and the cops let him take it. It was Joseph Hersch, calling from Chicago.

"Well, I guess I won't be living in the governor's mansion," Hersch said. "I was thinking, George. Maybe you could issue a new set of collector cards ... the Harry Jerome Conspiracy Edition. They'd sell like hotcakes. Of course, I'd expect a twenty percent royalty."

"You're out of your ever-lovin' mind!" Madden roared.

Nick Burnbaum shuffled into the police station and spotted the two reporters.

"Nice work, kids," he muttered.

"You were there when we needed you," Marilyn said.

"That's my job."

He started off, then turned around. "You know, Marilyn—with the big bucks you'll be making at the *Chronicle* you can afford to take cooking lessons."

He winked, then headed over to talk to policemen accompanying the conspirators.

Marilyn put her arms around McGraw. "We did it, McGraw."

"We sure did," he said.

Marilyn kissed him.

"And I want to congratulate you on taking it like a man. I mean, when a woman runs circles around some male reporters, they go berserk, but I think you came to realize I was the best reporter."

"What?" McGraw's eyes opened wide as Marilyn marched toward the door. "You're joking, right? I mean, you know that's not true. You're just saying that to irritate me. Isn't that right? ... *Stop right there, Marilyn! Let's talk about this!"*

Later that day, McGraw called his old boss, Walter Boylan, at the *National Exposer* in Florida.

"When are you coming back, McGraw? You'll die of boredom in Chicago. Those papers don't know what to do with a good story. *This* is where the action is. Just this morning there was another Elvis sighting in the Everglades ..."

Suspense and romance as
three TV reporters battle for a
network anchor job during
the 1991 war on Iraq

The rollicking story of a
three-way fight for a
$2.5-million-a-year
anchor job as war rages
in Iraq in 1991.

The Anchor War

John Westin

A candidate plots to steal the presidency in the Electoral College

Nonfiction and Fiction Worth Reading

Available now at McNeilandRichards.com